ASK ME TO DANCE

First published by Muswell Press in 2018

Typeset by e-Digital Design Ltd.

Copyright © Sylvia Colley 2018

Printed and bound by CPI Group (UK) Ltd, Croydon CR04YY.

Verse 4 of the text of "I danced in the morning (Lord of the Dance)" (Sydney Carter 1915-2004), © 1963 Stainer& Bell Ltd, 23 Gruneisen Road, London N3 1DZ, England, www.stainer.co.uk is used by kind permission. All rights reserved

This book is a work of fiction and, except in the case of historical fact, any resemblence to actual persons, living or dead, is purely coincidental.

A CIP catalogue record for this book is available from the British Library

ISBN 9781999811709

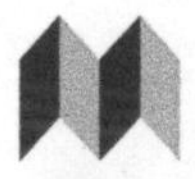

Muswell Press
London
N6 5HQ

www.muswell-press.co.uk

All rights reserved; no part of this publication may be reproduced, stored in a retrieval system, or transmitted in any form or by any means, electronic, mechanical, photocopying, recording, or otherwise without the prior written permission of the Publisher. This book may not be lent, resold, hired out or otherwise disposed of by way of trade in any form of binding or cover other than that in which it is published, without the prior written consent of the Publisher.

No responsibility for loss occasioned to any person or corporate body acting or refraining to act as a result of reading material in this book can be accepted by the Publisher, by the Author, or by the employer of the Author.

ASK ME TO DANCE

Sylvia Colley

To my daughter, Catherine,
and in memory of her sisters Juliet and Victoria

Chapter 1

I wasn't really listening. It was just a habit I'd got into, putting on the radio. It numbed the silence, that hum hum of voices. But I wasn't listening, just concentrating on the journey.

I was lucky with the weather – a clear, blue June day, the sun warm through the window – but I was anxious about making this journey alone, and had hardly slept, as I didn't know the way and was relying on the map and the scrawled address stapled to it. But now that I was on my way I felt unexpectedly buoyant, proud of myself and decided to stop for a coffee and cigarette. Cigarettes were a comfort. Of course, it shouldn't have been like this. Not like this at all. If things had gone as they should have, like in the normal life you expect and kind of take for granted – so stupidly, of course – Peter and the kids would have been here. Anyway, I wouldn't have been going alone to a monastery. We'd have been going on holiday somewhere or having a day out. But that was not how things had worked out and I was ill and the doctor had organised the whole thing. A retreat, they called it and I didn't argue, because I didn't care that much one way or the other. It took less energy just to go along with things.

My hands were sweaty with gripping the steering wheel too hard and I needed a loo, so when I saw a roadside café, a kind of truck-drivers' place, I pulled into the parking lot at the side. It was a prefabricated hut, really, but with a blue-and-white awning over a couple of white plastic tables with chairs. No one outside, but inside a group of truckers I guessed, all familiar with the place and each other. They stared at me and I gave a nod, confident that I looked OK in the green jeans and white blouse. Vanity, in spite of everything. You could laugh!

Two girls stood behind a counter with glass cases protecting various cakes and scones from the odd fly and wasp that hung around.

I asked about the ladies and the tallest of the two pointed. 'Outside and round the back. Round the back there,' she said. She was most likely doing a Saturday job; too young to have left school.

When I returned, I saw the coffee on a table near the men. They looked up vacantly as I picked it up and took it outside. The tabletop was cracked and pretty grimy and I did wonder whether anyone ever bothered to sit outside with the passing traffic and petrol fumes. But I could smoke and think and be alone, which is what I wanted just then. I wasn't alone for long though, as a grey four-by-four pulled up and the man and woman inside studied the café, the woman turning to say something to the three children in the back. In the end, they all got out and the children ran inside calling for ice cream and Coke. I watched as the woman opened her bag and handed the man money. I smiled as they passed and raised my eyebrows as if to say, 'I know! Been there! Got the T-shirt!'

They went to the other table, the man asking if he could take the spare chairs from mine. The children shrieked and fidgeted, slipping off their chairs to chase around the table. The woman leaned towards the man and he grabbed the youngest child and swung him onto his knee. The woman called, 'Come here, Paul, and drink your Coke,' and the boy dragged his sister to the table. I could hear the woman's quiet tones as she bent towards her husband and he took out a handkerchief and wiped the face of the wriggling child. I couldn't help staring at them, couldn't take my eyes off them, but they were too wrapped up in themselves to notice me.

I thought, What the hell am I doing here? Who is this sitting here quiet and alone? Moving on, moving on through time. The body moving; the self somewhere else.

I finished the coffee and went in to pay. Simple. Why bother to mention paying, except, you see, I couldn't find the right money in my purse. I knew it was there, that I had enough, but I couldn't make out £1.25. I couldn't work it out, so, panicking, I took out a £10 note instead.

Then the trembling started and the vague feeling of foreboding overcame me again, so I sat in the car and lit another cigarette and took deep breaths and all that stuff and wanted to go home, to my childhood home. I wanted my father. Wanted my father! Ever heard of a grown woman saying that? Anyway, I just sat there until the panic passed well enough for me to get on my way.

I missed the turning to the monastery, going up and down the winding lane several times. I had expected to see a large name announcing the place, but in fact there was simply a small metal sign swinging from a post, almost hidden by the branches of an overhanging tree. In faded white paint it read *Burnham Abbey*, with an arrow underneath, pointing towards a narrow driveway. I turned the car into the unmade track, dark in the shadows of heavy-leafed maple trees.

I came across the abbey suddenly; it stood in sunshine, long and white and deserted. The car was throbbing intrusively in the stillness, seemed so loud; I had the urge to just stop and walk, but I shouted at myself. I do shout out loud sometimes. Then I shouted, 'Get a bloody grip, you stupid cow. There's nothing to be anxious about.' And so, I drove up to the flagged area outside the front door.

It was very quiet once I had turned off the engine. Not a sound. No one about. I wasn't sure whether to take my stuff out of the car or to knock first, just to make sure they really were expecting me.

Then I heard a cuckoo echoing from a distance; a hollow reed, bell-like and persistent and that lovely sound carried with it memories of sun blowing through blue cotton curtains in that other life when the cuckoo call symbolised long, hot summer days. We had followed the call once, me and the children, and saw the cuckoo high in the elm tree the other side of the river.

I opened the boot and pulled out my holdall and a carrier bag filled with my sketch pads, paints and brushes, because I had imagined gardens like French chateau gardens and thought I would be able to find beautiful and secluded spots where I could paint, but I left the easel behind because I thought it might all seem a bit much. I shoved my battered straw hat onto the back of my head.

You could tell the place was badly run down, for the huge front door, which must have been magnificent once, was covered in feathered, flaking green paint and the doorknob was black with tarnish. I knew they were closing down soon, relocating to join another monastery in Wiltshire somewhere, yet were still taking visitors. Or so I thought. It would be like a hotel with a few prayers now and then. People would be charming and friendly and I would possibly make new friends. That's what I thought.

My hands full, I managed to push the bell with my chin, but nobody answered. I felt so alone. Helpless. Unsure what to do. In the end, I put down my stuff and opened the door. Obviously, like churches, the doors remained unlocked during the day. I pushed my way in and piled my luggage against a wall, my hat on top, and stood in the shadows by the door.

In the great square hall with its wooden floors and dust-covered table, the smell caught me by surprise, reminding me of school dinners, that sickening, tepid smell of boiled fish. I was shocked. There were two doors, one either side of the hall, both shut, but, wherever it was coming from, the smell of cooking was heavy in the air. Yet opposite me, French windows opened onto lawns, yellow in the sunlight, where surely the air would be fresh.

On the right was the long, dusty table with books on it and a brass bell, and there I saw a faded notice propped against the bell, which read *Please ring.*

I couldn't bring myself to ring the bell immediately, the sound shocking the silence, so I stood for a while looking out of the windows at the lawns that sloped up and away from the house and at the trees surrounding the lawns: beech, oak and blue-black cypress.

Still no one came, so I knew I had to ring the bell, deciding that if this brought no one, I was definitely going home. Then suddenly, making me jump, a door on the right opened and this tiny figure appeared, shuffling towards me. He looked grubby and unkempt, his brown habit marked with food stains, and he wore slippers. He came up so close, his breath hot and sour in my face, all the time grinning at me. I felt him touching me. I didn't like it and moved away. He smelled of fish and dirt and I thought he was revolting.

'They're all in chapel.' he shouted. 'But I'm in the kitchen.'

'I'm Rose Gregory. I've booked in for a few days.'

But he wasn't listening, kept turning his head towards the door as if he was doing something wrong, as if he was expecting someone to come through the door.

'Mustn't let Francis come in here.' And he exhaled a long hum, shaking his head, still grinning. 'Not allowed.' And he shook his head backwards and forwards with a, 'No No No!' He turned to me. 'It's fish today. Should have been Friday but the delivery didn't come in time.' He gave a kind of choke. 'So, we're having it today instead. Father is not pleased.' Then he turned to go, calling back, 'Have you come for lunch?'

My nervousness was beginning to turn to rage. 'I've come to stay. I arranged it with Father Godfrey a week ago.'

Suddenly he seemed to understand but said nothing, just shuffled past me and through the French windows. I had no idea what I was supposed to do, so I picked up all my bits and pieces and followed him. He turned round to look at me but didn't speak.

'Am I supposed to be following you?' I called, but he just shunted onwards, mumbling to himself.

I thought, God help me. I've come to a lunatic asylum. I want wisdom. Guidance. Healing. But I've come to a lunatic asylum. Ah well. We can all be mad together.

He turned around as he was hurrying. 'It's just you.'

'Just me what?' I had imagined visitors sitting in deckchairs in the garden, reading, talking to each other, walking together into meals, smiling with recognition. I could not believe I was going to be alone amongst these peculiar monks. All alone.

We crossed the lawn to the left and turned down a path, which wound through overgrown rhododendrons, heavy with blossoms, emerging to reveal a low prefabricated building surrounded by a cracked and weedy concrete path. The quivering monk opened one of the doors on the long side of the building, looked inside, and then shut it again. His head was continually nodding and he seemed rather agitated. 'Not that one. We don't get many these days.'

It was the third door that he finally opened and let me through. The sunlight caught the stubble on his face as he watched me like a curious child. His faded blue eyes watered.

'How long are you staying?' he asked, and he grinned before turning away, not waiting for my answer, mumbling something about a rabbit.

He was like one of the dwarfs in *Snow White*. I watched him, head poking forward like a chicken, arms hanging stiffly, as he half ran, half skipped down the path and out of sight. And I stayed there in the doorway and wanted to cry, but, 'You mustn't cry,' Mother had said. 'You must never cry.'

I didn't want to go into my room and shut the door. Somehow. But I did, of course, because there was nothing else I could do. It was a small room with an iron bedstead, striped ticking mattress and a pile of bedding neatly folded at one end. It reminded me of boarding school. There was a threadbare rug by the bed and on the other side of the room a dark oak table with a Bible and a wooden crucifix on the wall above it. Opposite the bed stood a modern teak chest of drawers, and across the far corner a flowered chintz curtain, which I guessed was some makeshift wardrobe. My stuff had fallen and was spread over the floor, so I had to step over it to investigate. I was right. Behind the curtain was a rail with a few wooden hangers. There was no washbasin or loo, though. No ensuite! To be honest, it was about as bad as it could get. So where was the bathroom? I discovered it two doors down. Yellow walls, cork bath mat propped up against the side of the bath, and a canister of Vim with a blue J-cloth standing in the white basin. The only good thing about it all was as there were apparently no others staying, I would have the bathroom to myself. That was one thing at least.

I did manage to shove a few things away and make up the bed but, that done, I pulled the green velvet curtains, faded round the edges, across the windows to keep out the glaring sun and got under the blanket, pulled it over my head to shut out the light and tried to escape into sleep.

I hadn't brought any photographs; just the snapshots in the back of my wallet. Photos were like crying. How hopeless to think crying could do anything. I liked the snapshots because the kids were smiling and happy. They had been happy, hadn't they? But, with them gone, tears were trivial, almost an insult. It can't be explained; only that there were four of us and now there's just me. It's really very simple. And the thing is, I don't feel anything any more. No, it's true. I absolutely don't. Not proud of it, but there it is. If someone I knew, a friend say, came and told me that their kids had been killed in a plane disaster, I wouldn't feel anything. I would be very sorry. Very sorry indeed, but I wouldn't *feel* sorry. There is a difference. Am I psychopathic? I must be. No feelings, you see. So, I don't cry and I didn't bring any photos.

Chapter 2

Father Godfrey, Abbot of Burnham Abbey, looked at his watch; nearly an hour to lunch and he was already peckish. 'I'll put on weight if I'm not careful. Not good. Not good at all,' he said to himself. He returned to the letter he was writing to his friend, Father Julian, Abbot of Wiltdown, about their move there. Details of this and that to be settled.

He leaned back in his chair and stared out at the gardens, the cedar tree and yes, as usual the rabbit was tied to the rope there, and nibbling away. He knew something had to happen in that department but preferred just now to put it out of his mind. Too many other things going on. They had this woman to deal with. What was her name? He found a piece of paper on which he had written *Mrs Rose Gregory, arriving Saturday 10th June.* He thought, Must remember her name: never been good at names – and getting worse.

He had no idea what they should do with her. Their only visitor. Her doctor – what was his name? – happened to be a colleague of their Dr Guy and knew from him about Burnham Abbey, the fact that they took visitors, and had phoned himself, explaining everything he could and asking that they keep an eye on her, adding that all she wanted was peace and quiet. Well, she would certainly get that here! But a woman alone! That was most awkward, very awkward indeed. But poor woman. What must it have been like to stand helpless, as in a split second both children, young children, were knocked down by a car. He thought that's what the doctor said. Was it possible to recover from something like that? And then her husband leaving. Probably to escape the grief. Men were never very good with grief. His mind turned to Brother Joseph's grief after the death of Brother John. He sighed with weariness and, putting his elbows on the desk, held his head in his hands. 'Oh yes! A dreadful situation,' he said aloud, but probably it was best to leave her alone. We all have to find our own way in the end.

Now he felt helpless and lethargic. He had enough problems with all this moving business. Thirty-two years here; it was home. He looked back at the gardens, remembering the early days when there was a full complement of brothers, and money was not so tight. Then they kept the gardens in excellent shape and the vegetable gardens supplied the locals, who came regularly to buy fresh produce and eggs too. They had chickens where the dogs' run is now, and bees. Their honey was well known in the area. But it was so different now; only eleven of them and no money, of course, to keep the place going, as they naturally had little support from the Church. And so, the amalgamation with Wiltdown. But it could be worse. Father Julian and he had trained together all those years ago, became friends and kept in touch. And in so many ways it would be a relief to have someone else in charge.

But what would happen to this place? Had been a grand – beautiful even – house. He supposed the builders would be all over it in five minutes. The house pulled down and the gardens probably covered in blocks of flats. Only the graveyard: that couldn't be built on, for sure. Not hallowed ground. Oh well, it was not his problem and there was nothing he could do. But the graves must be left alone. Of course, it was possible someone might renovate the place and turn it into and old people's home. He quite liked that idea. Perhaps one day he could move back himself!

Chapter 3

As I lay there with my eyes closed, I tried to regain my sense of positive reality, but I couldn't. I thought, My body goes on automatically, but myself is somewhere else. I could see myself only as one remembers an old photograph; there was no more connection than that. I thought, No one understands that the real me is standing, waiting on another path. Then I said to myself, But I am living. It is me. It's no one else. The hard work and the mistakes are mine; the friendships, the laughter, the fear and the despair are mine and the exhaustion is mine. And yet it was unreal to me. I was insubstantial, standing and watching myself. I often thought that if I could have just one long, deep sleep, the blissful sleep of a child, I'd be OK.

When I was very little, someone took my hand and led me to see the baby lying in his crib. My brother, Duncan. He lay with his face on one side, eyes tight shut, far away, peaceful, and I loved him.

'Shh,' someone said. 'You'll wake the baby.' And for days after that, so I've been told, I went around with my finger over my lips saying, 'Shh! Baba cries.' Instinctively, I knew then that by loving the baby, by caring for the baby, I could become part of the baby and then Mother would not forget me. Mother would love me too. Why did I always feel that I had to please to be loved? Because that way I would survive? By loving, by pleasing: then I became substantial. Had I not loved and pleased I would have faded into the outer edges of people's consciousness and disappeared. I was always terrified of disappearing, of being unseen. Being unseen is worse than being alone.

Mother seemed to notice me when I was clever and pretty, loved me when I sang and danced, because I was more pretty and clever than the other children.

'Ask me to dance, Mummy.'

Mother was proud of me then and arranged rather grand birthday parties, and I would have a new dress and dance and sing.

Once, I had a birthday party – perhaps I was six or seven – and Granny made me a very special taffeta dress, all orange and shiny. I loved it but hated being fitted for it; couldn't keep still.

Lots of people I didn't know were invited and Mother hired a hall, and an old lady, wearing a hat with a feather in it, played the piano and I danced, and sang in front of all the guests 'I'll Be With You in Apple Blossom Time'. I wasn't shy or afraid then but spun about the polished floor in black patent shoes and the orange taffeta dress, while solemn-faced mothers and their children watched. They seemed disapproving, somehow. Was I too precocious? But Mother looked proud.

At another party, still with children and mothers I didn't know, for I only had two friends, Margaret Cousins and Pamela Riddle, I won a game of musical chairs. Then a thin, pale, bony girl with a mousy fringe, who continually hung on to her mother's arm, whined and cried because she wanted to have my mystery present wrapped in red crepe paper with its suggestion of Christmas surprises. I couldn't believe it when, without warning, Mother took the present out of my hands and gave it to the snivelling child instead. I can still remember my humiliation – the humiliation of the very public revelation that Mother did not stick up for me, was more bothered about the other girl, who was loved by her own mother, and my shame was followed by blind fury. How at that moment I hated the stupid, snivelling child whose mother so openly adored her; this stupid child's mother loved her for all the world to see. I snatched back the present, the prize that was rightfully mine and then Mother took hold of me in front of all of them, saying, 'You're a very naughty girl,' and dragged me off to my bedroom. Then, locking the door behind me, she left me to my fury and misery.

I knelt by the bed, sobbing and hating Mother because, although I could not have put words to it, I understood that her image as a gracious hostess was more important than justice for me. And I had to pay her back. I would not be outdone. I would make her sorry. And so I found a pack of playing cards and spread them all over the floor, all over my bed, the chair, on top of the chest of drawer. It seemed then a terrifyingly naughty thing to do. But that would teach Mother not to favour other children before me. I sat on the edge of the bed, swinging my legs defiantly.

Mother remembered me after a while and I was so happy to hear her footsteps that I forgot the cards.

'Are you sorry?' she called through the door.

No answer.

'Are you going to be good now?'

No answer.

She opened the door, saw the cards spread over the room, slammed the door and shouted, 'You can come out when you have picked all those up.'

Memories. I sat up suddenly, remembering, always remembering my life was only memories, and leaned against the iron bedstead and the room moved like water as the shadows from the trees outside swayed to and fro in front of the sun. There was no ashtray, of course, so I would have to use the top of my face-cream jar. Smoking was probably forbidden here; people in monasteries don't need props like tobacco. These people have found their way to peace and fulfilment without treats. But if God wanted me, He would have to find me; He would have to take the trouble. It was up to Him. I thought, I've been naive to have so much faith. But not any more.

Oh no! I wouldn't make the same mistake twice. If God was there, then He could find me. Nothing I could do.

There was that midday silence, the silence of loneliness. I was not used to silence and wished I had brought a radio with me. The cuckoo had stopped. His moment was short-lived. It was the same with butterflies who were born and then died in the same day. I had often noticed how active they were and then how suddenly still, how they fluttered quiveringly and frantically one minute and then rested so quietly the next. They never knew they were being watched, but I had watched them as in pairs they copulated on the wing, and I knew that, in a sense, their acts of loving were their death throes, for shortly afterwards they would die. Opposites. Love and hate, life and death, light and dark. Fleur had loved butterflies. We had spent hours together, butterfly-spotting, yet only once had she seen a blue butterfly. Strangely, I have seen them quite often since. They seemed to be returning to the gardens once again, but when Fleur was searching we had to go to the Dorset coast and the Sussex Downs. And just once we saw one! There it was, suddenly, a touch of pure blue as we followed it hovering through the long summer grasses. We had been so excited.

One of my childish obsessions had been wanting to fly like a butterfly or a bird. For hours at a time I would stand on the dining-room table, trying desperately hard to fly off it. I would work my arms frantically and, when I was dizzy with the effort, would leap into the air, arms flapping madly, but although the floor seemed such a long way down, I always hit it just too soon for lift-off. Only once, for an ecstatic moment, did I think I had succeeded, and it happened to be when I was demonstrating to Duncan. Then I really did, just for a moment, seem to hover, seemed to fly. 'I flew! I flew! I really flew, Duncan! Did you see me? Did you see me fly?'

Duncan seemed unusually impressed and decided to fly himself, but he jumped too high and too far without any care, and fell onto a chair and broke his nose. There was blood everywhere and an awful rumpus. And I was blamed. Nobody actually said so, but I perceived their cold eyes and their concern for my bleeding brother.

The Angelus rang three or four times, as if calling. Was I supposed to do something? I didn't mind staying where I was, provided I could sleep, but to be awake and do nothing, that was intolerable. What would Dan and Fleur have to say? I always thought: only Dan and Fleur can make it right. Fleur would say what she always said when things got tricky. For instance, if I was trying to unravel an impossibly knotted piece of her knitting or trying to nurture a throbbing baby bird, then Fleur would say, 'Don't give up, Mum. You won't give up, will you?'

Once when I was in the kitchen crying over a TV news item about foster child who was literally dragged away from the only parents she knew, Fleur, all of five years old, stamped into the kitchen and, standing feet apart and hands on hips, as was her habit, shouted derogatively, 'Well, don't just stand there crying. Do something!'

And so I did. I wrote, like thousands of others, to the Home Office and got a reply, which assured me that there were going to be changes to the law that would prevent such a thing happening again. I wouldn't have written that letter if it hadn't been for Fleur. Daniel, in contrast, would say nothing, but would just be there watching, quiet and resolute. I could feel his support, although, like his dad, he didn't say much. I didn't need the photos to remember Dan with his pale, thoughtful face and Fleur, the green-eyed pixie, with soft brown freckles on her nose.

I didn't cry. I sat up in the bed and wondered if I'd loved them enough. Whether I'd ever been capable of love, if I even knew what love was. What is love, actually? But I knew why I was in this place. In truth, I had died when they died. Only you couldn't tell. Nobody knew, for the shell still hung on the tree and you couldn't know it was split and that the kernel, the life force, had disappeared. Gone. Died. You couldn't see the shell was empty.

Chapter 4

I must have been dreaming, because a persistent knocking at a door brought me back to the room, the place. I stumbled to open the door, black spots spinning before my eyes and my heart pounding. A monk stood outside. His young face was red and blotched with spots and his head completely shaven. He stood tall and thin and gazed down at me with a straight back.

'It's lunch, 'he said. 'Lunch is at twelve-thirty.'

'Oh! What's the time then?'

'You're late. It's nearly twenty to. Everyone's waiting.' He looked down at me crossly, as if waiting for me to say something.

'Sorry. I didn't know. Can you show me where to go, please? I don't know where to go.'

I didn't want any lunch; I looked at the spots oozing round his neck and felt sick. He probably picked them. Disgusting. I prayed he would not be anywhere near me.

I asked if I had time to wash my hands. I wanted to tidy my hair and put on some make-up. Vanity? I wanted to look as well as possible; it gave me confidence, helped me to be cheerful. Helped me to be 'frightfully jolly' as my grandmother would say. Besides, it was a kind of duty. I believe everyone should try to look as good as possible, to hide the world's ugliness, the world's brutality. Grey people only contribute to life's greyness, do nothing to wipe the smile off the face of the satanic tiger. But there was no time, the brother said, for we were already late and so I followed the spotty 'Buddhist' monk as he led the way back across the lawn to the house.

Once in the lobby, I followed him through the door, from which the little monk had appeared earlier, and into a gloomy corridor. A little way down a shaft of light, falling across the wooden floor, indicated an open door.

I asked him 'In here?' in as interested tone as I could manage, but my voice echoed sharp as a knife. He nodded and I went in behind him.

Everything was silent. The monks were standing behind their chairs, waiting. The young monk pointed to an empty place at one of the long tables.

I said, 'Thank you,' before realising I wasn't supposed to speak. I thought they seemed a bit disturbed and I was embarrassed and relieved to be able to lower my head for grace. 'For what we are about to receive may we give thanks and praise always. In the name of the Father, the Son and the Holy Spirit. Amen.'

There were no answering 'Amens', simply a scraping of chairs as they all sat. For one moment, I thought the monk to my left, a large, flabby, red-faced man, was courteously waiting for me to sit first, and I smiled warmly, gratefully, but he was only waiting because I had caught the leg of my chair in his habit and he looked at me with impatience as I wrestled with the chair legs.

Once seated, everyone waited in silence as a good-looking monk, dark-haired, of middle age, stepped onto a rostrum in the far corner of the room and began to read, but no one appeared to be listening. Three other monks gathered by a serving hatch and almost at once hands, from the kitchen, passed through bowls and I caught sight of the little monk,who had shown me to my room peering, grinning, from the other side of the hatch. I was sure he was grinning at me so I looked away.

There were three tables forming a rectangle, and at the table opposite I was surprised by a man, not a monk, sitting at the end. He was wearing a blue polo shirt under a tweed jacket. He looked perfectly at home; everything about him told me he was not a visitor. There was something reassuring about him and I wanted to know more, but when he looked across with a half-smile of welcome I turned my head away, suddenly shy, and focused on the top table, assuming that the stately looking monk sitting in the middle must be the abbot, Father Godfrey. He was served first by the young monk who had come to fetch me. The bowls contained a thick brown soup, rather cold, and this was followed by fish, yellow and curled up at the edges, accompanied by mashed potato and pale, watery sprouts. They all ate with fierce concentration, looking neither to left nor right. While they waited for the empty plates to be removed, to be replaced by stewed apples and custard, the monks simply stared into space. It was as if I didn't exist.

I had fiddled with the fish but left the sprouts and potato and shook my head when the spotty monk offered me the pudding. There were bowls of fruit on the tables, oranges and apples, and I took an apple when the disgruntled monk beside me pushed a bowl in my direction.

When everyone had finished eating and the plates were cleared, the stately monk rose and left the room, then all the others filed out, top table first, just like school. I hesitated, but the monk who had offered me the fruit nodded when I looked questioningly at him and so I followed in line. It was the same important ritual, the same important order, as when I lined up for communion. Everyone must be in his right place or else the whole edifice of doctrine would apparently collapse.

As they exited, the monks hurried towards the entrance-hall door and disappeared, while the man who had smiled at me walked down the corridor past the kitchen in the opposite direction, and so I found myself retracing my steps alone.

Chapter 5

Normally, after lunch Guy Harwood went for a walk. He liked a walk, and the ancient wood, not more than ten minutes away, was his favourite, for it had, probably centuries ago, been planted with beech and oaks which now were great trees spreading their branches across the well-worn tracks.

His self-contained flat was at the far end of the Abbey, away from the others, which pleased him, for he preferred to be alone. The flat consisted of his small surgery and then, through a series of adjoining doors, his sitting room, the bedroom and bathroom. He had been given permission to give it all a coat of paint, pale grey, and he had brought a few personal bits: his chair, piano and books.

Now he sat at the piano and without much thought began to play by heart a Mozart minuet. The woman looked nervous, ill at ease, he thought. Not really surprising – the only woman among men! She hadn't eaten properly, perhaps that was why she was so slim. Looked as if a breath of air could blow her over. She wasn't beautiful, but he had to admit that for him there was something lovely about her. So pale. Chestnut hair bundled up with loose bits hanging down her neck. He had had a long chat with Tom about her, so he knew the situation. Wasn't really sure what he was supposed to do, however. Tom had said he hoped the break away somewhere peaceful would help; he wanted to try that before resorting to anti-depressants. But she was stubborn, apparently. Well, he would definitely have to find an occasion to meet her. What would happen after that? He didn't know. He could help build her confidence, perhaps?

All he knew was he didn't want any serious involvement and he could detect in himself the warning signs. But no. Not after Elizabeth.

He had met her and Tom when they, all three, were training together at Barts, had become great friends and all gone to Bristol General as junior doctors, where they met up in pubs after shifts, gave each other lifts to and from their digs, went to parties, the cinema and discussed endlessly the pros and cons of life as junior doctors.

Then Tom met Di, and he and Elizabeth saw less of him and were, in a way, thrown together. Elizabeth was petite with a fuzz of naturally curly brown hair and, like him, she wore glasses. When their friendship developed into something more intimate, they used to joke, 'You're steaming up my glasses!'

He thought they would never be apart. But could not decide how they would be together either. Kissing was OK, but he couldn't do the sex bit. Too afraid. He'd masturbate alone after being with her, imagining her all the time, her plumpish thighs, her breasts.

He supposed he should have known. Yet when she told him that evening in the restaurant, one of their favourite places, that she had met somebody who made her feel a woman, where the chemistry was good, he was stunned into a shaking silence. Took him years to get over it.

All the time Tom remained a good friend, as did Di, whom he married shortly after Guy's break-up with Elizabeth. Guy saw a lot of them, especially as he and Tom became partners in the same practice. And he was looking forward, after this sabbatical, to working alongside Tom again. He would leave here when the rest moved to Wiltdown, staying, of course, to help with the move.

In the meantime, he should walk, not think about Rose Gregory, despite the fact that there was something about her that he was drawn to. But no! Never again. He shut the lid of the piano, took out a handkerchief and cleaned his glasses, sat for a moment, thinking, and then left for his walk.

Chapter 6

When I re-entered the hall, the monk I assumed to be the abbot was waiting for me. He smiled politely but wearily.

'Mrs Gregory.' He held out his hand. 'I'm sorry I wasn't here to welcome you on arrival; I was saying Matins.'

'Oh! Not to worry. I was well looked after.' I wanted to look 'frightfully jolly'. 'I think I was early, anyway.' It was me trying to put him at his ease! 'I wasn't quite sure how long the journey would take. It was quicker than I expected.'

'No trouble. No trouble.' And he tried to copy my cheerfulness. 'But I'm afraid we have to keep rather strict times here. Everyone gets very thrown out if we go astray in that department.'

He was a tall, slim upright man with a mass of white hair, a strand of which fell over his eyes, and now and again he would push it out of the way. His face was tanned and there was a youthful light in his eyes, despite the deep furrows that ran from either side of his long, straight nose. The continual movement of his arms as he swung them from behind his back to his sides and the regular flicking of his fingers as he ran them round and round across the palms of his hands signified some agitation, I thought, but he looked like an abbot. Something at least was how I had imagined it to be. I thought, Here is someone I might be able to talk to.

'You've found your quarters all right?'

'Yes, thank you. One of the brothers – small man – said something about a rabbit?'

'Oh! The rabbit! Yes, that's Brother Joseph,' he said with a hint of irritation. And then, changing the subject, 'They're nice apartments, aren't they? We had them built some years ago. But, as I explained to your doctor on the telephone, we've rather stopped having visitors, as we're getting ready to move. All very sad, but there are so few of us now. We can't afford the upkeep any more. Well, there it is. I won't bore you with all our troubles.' And he gave a weary smile. 'Now look,' he went on, 'We all have a quiet time now, reading and so on, but if you'd like to come back here at three, I'll take you round the gardens. Or have you explored them already?'

'No. Not yet. But I'd like to. What I've seen so far all looks very nice. Must be a lot of work.'

'Well, then I expect you would like to see them. They used to be our pride and joy. But that's another thing we can't keep as we would like. Never mind. Never mind.' But he did mind and I could see his attention was already moving away from me and on to more pressing matters.

'However,' – he obviously thought he should make some effort with me, and he pointed towards the door on the right of the hall – 'let me show you our library. We do have a very good stock of books. Our visitors often give us books too. You do read, I suppose?' And he looked at me with what I think was a quick wink.

'Of course.' I tried a laugh.

'Well, come along with me, then.' And he led the way through the door on the opposite side of the entrance hall and almost immediately through another on the right.

It was a huge room with long windows that looked out onto the garden; the rest of the walls were lined with books from floor to ceiling. There were several small tables around which were two or three chairs and at two of the tables now sat three of the brothers, two at one table and one at the other. One momentarily glanced up with a blank gaze, but the others continued reading.

'We don't talk in here,' Father Godfrey whispered. 'You can read in here if you wish, but I expect you'd prefer to go back to your quarters. Have a look around; you may find something to interest you. We do have some very fine books.' He waved his arm towards the shelves. 'I'll meet you back here at three. Now, I must go and do some office work.' And then, whispering closely, 'It's one of the more distasteful aspects of this job.' He nodded goodbye and left, shutting the door very quietly. Don't know why, but I had the distinct feeling that he was going to have a nap.

Chapter 7

I immediately turned away from the reading brothers and made a good pretence of examining the books. The last time I had been looking at books in my local library, I experienced that frightening mental block – you know, couldn't remember what I was looking for and none of the titles seemed to make sense. God, I was scared witless. It was a bit the same in the monastery library. I couldn't take anything in and not having my glasses with me didn't help. My eyes are always bad when I'm tired or a bit stressed. Perhaps that was it. Still, I had to pick a book, as I was sure that I was being studied from behind.

Many of the books were seriously old and yet, incongruously, now and again I would see a bright modern novel. There was P.D. James's *The Black Tower*, a thriller that Peter had borrowed from me to read one summer holiday. Extraordinary for a book like that to be in a monastic library. Pete had said it was good. There must have been more to it than I had realised. I respected his opinion on books. Perhaps, if I took the book off the shelf and then turned around quickly, he would be there. I often had absurd dreams like that.

One recurring fantasy was that one day I would open the front door and find them standing there or they would come upon me suddenly, silently as I was gardening. I had to be gardening, had to be absorbed – expecting nothing. They would come when I was least expecting it. It's mad, I know, but I couldn't help it. I looked for then in shops, in the streets, even some days when I walked out of the hospital where I worked, wondering if they might be there to greet me. And of course, last thing at night I imagined what it would be like to come across them without warning. I knew that at the moment of reunion my heart could not sustain the joy, and as I thought of it my chest would literally ache. What Mary must have felt in the garden of Gethsemane. Unimaginable joy. She was lucky. I loathe Easter now.

Most of the books were on religious and spiritual themes: *The True Way*, *The Art of Meditation*. I had cared about those sorts of things once. But now I challenged God just as I had challenged Mother after she had unjustly locked me in my room. I was waiting for something, with my 'legs swinging defiantly' and the 'cards of revenge' lay all around me.

It was the rage. I deliberately dropped a book on the floor. The crash reverberated round the silence. I didn't turn to see the effect but I hoped they, poor deluded souls, had jumped out of their skins. After I had replaced the book on the shelf I turned and whispered a loud, 'Sorry.' The monks lifted their eyes and I grinned at them, as if to say, 'Aren't I careless?' I wasn't angry with them, really; I knew I couldn't be angry with anyone, not even God. That's the problem. There's no one to blame. That's the fucking trouble.

I felt tired. I wanted to go back to my 'apartment' when I saw a book I had at home and knew well, because Matthew, my fatal attraction, had given it to me for my twenty-first birthday. *The Letters of Luke, the Physician*, written by Canon Rogers, my school chaplain. What would Canon Rogers say to me now, I wondered? Would he think I had failed 'to keep the flag flying'? It was his pet expression and it made the other girls laugh. When I said my final farewell to him he said, 'You will keep the flag flying, won't you?' And I had promised I would try. That was because we were alone in his study. Had the other girls been there I would have mumbled something innocuous. They already thought of me as 'terribly religious' and as 'his pet', and I hated that. I didn't want to be different; I wanted to be one of the girls.

The trouble was that Canon Rogers was a very odd-looking man. He had been, rumour had it, dreadfully tortured by the Japanese during the war and this had left him with a severe nervous tic; his head continually rolled from side to side, as if he had cerebral palsy. His whole appearance reminded one of a rag doll: spineless, floppy, uncontrollable, and the girls mimicked him cruelly. I had treated him badly: run away from him if he was coming my way, avoided him, laughed with the others about him behind his back; all this to disguise the bond and understanding that lay between us, which kind of frightened me. He had understood my tempestuous nature, warned me that life, for me, would be full of ups and downs. He had known, seen it coming in some extraordinary way. But he was dead now and I was sorry about that because I knew that despite my juvenile cruelty, he had loved me. I couldn't handle being loved. I didn't recognise it at all. Matthew understood about this bond and that was why he gave me the book.

I heard a door shut and turned to find the monk who had been sitting alone had gone. The other two still seemed to be engrossed in their reading, although I felt they had been watching me while my back was turned. I took the book off the shelf and left the library. Perhaps I would read it again, but for the moment all I wanted was to lie down and sleep. The last hour had exhausted me.

Chapter 8

Father Godfrey put his signature to the letter and leaned back in his chair. He pushed the strand of hair out of his eyes, took off his glasses, rubbed his hands over his forehead and yawned. He was always tired after lunch. Lunch had been a disappointment today; he really would have to speak to Brother Joseph about his work in the kitchen. But it was difficult to know how to deal with the man, for he was quite incapable of doing anything properly except looking after that darned rabbit. Yet he must have something to do; it was bad for him to do nothing; it was bad for anyone. Everyone should feel worthy at doing something.

Annoyingly, Brother Joseph was disarmingly content with himself, had no conception of his – dare Godfrey think it? – simple-mindedness. He had always been a problem, of course; all right if there was a definite set of rules to follow, but change the routine – well, then there was a to-do. Brother Joseph plodded through the routine he was used to, unaware of the others around him, peeling potatoes even if they were not required, warming plates even if it was salad. And the other brothers didn't help, mind you; they ganged up, whispering to each other, watching his mistakes and then laughing amongst themselves. Oh yes, he'd seen. But Joseph appeared oblivious to it all and that somehow made it all the more irritating.

Something had to be done: he would have to find him some other task. And one where hygiene didn't matter either! My goodness, what a state his clothes were in. He couldn't have someone in the community looking like that, especially now they were joining the brethren at Wiltdown. And, come to that, something had to be done about that rabbit. Why oh why had he allowed him to keep it? But he knew why. At the time, he had thought it fortuitous, with Joseph so distraught at Brother John's death. The rabbit filled the gap. Brought in by a cat, wasn't it? Anything to help him. He didn't enjoy the suffering of his fellow men and too often he felt helpless in the face of it. Joseph had been quite broken by his friend's death; they'd been together since they were boys; it had been pitiful to see. What did he call him? Billie? Yes, he called him Billie, but here it had been Brother John. Only the rabbit brought him comfort, it seemed.

At least, Godfrey thought, he will never suffer as Brother John did: he became so filled with a sense of his own futility, with a sense of a completely wasted life, that he had gone quite mad. Although they had let him breed spaniels, turned the chicken run into special kennels for the dogs, it only helped for a time. No, he had died the worst death of all; died in utter hopelessness, believing that God was a terrible hoax, some ghastly trick played on man by man. One could only hope that he had found peace at last.

He sighed, pushed back his chair and went to sit in the armchair by the window, hitching up his black robes to make himself more comfortable and revealing grey socks, with garters strapped to his white legs. He picked up a book from the table beside him and began to read, but as usual his eyes closed, the book fell into his lap and he dozed.

Once more he was walking through the garden in India. The air was close and still, brown air. Everything was brown and dust rose from his feet. Someone was singing. He kept muttering a text over and over again, but the words made no sense and he saw one of the servants grinning at him from behind the shrubbery. But when he looked again, the servant had gone. And then he saw the woman waiting at the end of the path; her chestnut hair shone rich in the sunlight, but her complexion was pale and, as he approached, he noticed how tired she looked. She stared at him with hollow eyes, but he walked past and when he turned around she had gone too. And he was sad, for she had seemed lonely and vulnerable standing there.

He woke suddenly and looked at his watch; it was ten to three. He knew he'd been dreaming about India again. He never used to. Never had dreamed about that part of this life before. Perhaps it was because he was old now. Perhaps one's mind pulled together all of one's life through dreams. On the other hand, perhaps it was because of the move. He was dreading it; he was to be as uprooted as, in a sense, he had uprooted himself from his family and India. Yes, that must be the reason he kept dreaming in this way.

It was nearly time to take the woman round the gardens. He didn't really know what else he could do. There was something about the woman in his dream that edged his mind and made him uncomfortable. Yet what could he do? And then he remembered the leaflet they always left in the apartments. Had she got one, he wondered. He moved back to his desk and, pulling open the long, central drawer, found a rather creased and battered pamphlet, which he tried to iron out on the sides of his robes. It would have to do. At least it told her the times of the services and meals as well as a few necessary dos and don'ts. Now it was time to go. Well, at least he would have done something.

Chapter 9

I couldn't sleep, so I smoked two cigarettes instead, lying back on the bed and shutting my eyes every now and again. I thought about Matthew and the book and the time he had told me he was considering entering a monastery. It had made me angry.

'Escaping again?'

'Not entirely.' He always refused to take my bait. He had understood me more than I understood him.

'Give me the reasons, then, though I'll never be convinced. I think it's a load of rubbish myself. The most awful cop-out.'

But he explained that for him prayer worked rather like telepathy. The thought waves of prayer went out and were picked up subconsciously by those minds that could act as receivers, in the way radio waves did.

'Concentrated prayer is only concentrated thoughts,' he said, 'and the results are never measurable. Who could tell where a thought comes from? All I know is that it is the only way things ever get done. Thank God for the transmitters!'

'And what about celibacy then?' I said. 'What's all that about?'

He laughed. He had such a generous, throaty laugh, full of kindness. 'Helps keep your mind on your work!'

'I should have thought it was quite the reverse,' I snapped. I wasn't very kind. 'Doesn't one always want what one can't have? As far as

I know, people who don't have sex think about it all the time.' He laughed again, refusing to be drawn. This was a delicate subject for us.

Matthew was the chaplain at Duncan's school and I first met him when Mother and I went to the annual school play. This particular year it was *As You Like It* and Duncan was playing Rosalind. We did laugh!

I had just left school, was eighteen and I can remember the bottle-green velvet coat I bought especially for the occasion. I will be honest and say that I realised the stir I caused amongst the boys and enjoyed it enormously. 'Have you seen Duncan's sister? Who is the girl in green?' Ever after that, apparently, I was referred to as 'the girl in green'.

It was there that I first met Matthew, at the reception after the play. Mother already knew him from other school occasions and made a beeline for him as the one really attractive man in the room. Mother liked men and flirted outrageously, a characteristic that made me squirm. Actually, Matthew at thirty-eight was nearer Mother's age than mine. In the event, it was odd that Mother, who quite obviously was attracted to him herself, should so blatantly have encouraged our relationship. It didn't strike me as odd at the time, only much later.Was it so that she could have just a little bit of him? Or did she know it would end in disaster for me? Can't ask her now, since she died of cancer soon after Dan was born. And no, I didn't cry, Mother. Remember you told me not to.

My first impression of Matthew was mixed. I have to admit that he was handsome: tall, blondish wavy hair, with startling blue eyes. The boys nicknamed him Bing or Old Blue Eyes after Bing Crosby because, besides his eyes, he had a good singing voice. But he annoyed me at that first meeting, liking himself a bit too much, playing on his charm and good looks as he tried to persuade Mother to allow Duncan to go with the sailing group he was organising. He must have known we couldn't afford it. There was something loose-lipped and pleading about his manner which irritated me, and perhaps our relationship would never have developed had Mother not taken an enormous bite out of a sticky bun, dislodged her lower dentures and been obliged to make a hasty retreat. Consequently, we were left alone together. Alone, that is, in the midst of a seething crowd of sons and parents and other teachers. But I was quite unaware of anyone else that evening as I stood looking up into his face with the penetrating blue eyes. I snapped at him nevertheless.

'Why are you pressing Mother so? You know we don't have much money now.'

'You're right,' he said. 'I apologise.' He had completely disarmed me. And then, looking down at me with that urgent expression I came to know so well, 'If I may say so, I hadn't realised that Duncan had such a beautiful sister. It will make all the boys jealous to see that I have you all to myself.'

I tried in vain to maintain my irritation, but the remark, it seemed to me then, was made sincerely and his speaking voice so deep and smooth. I fell for him.

It was several years, however, before I was to see him again. By then I was at St Mark's Hospital as one of several PAs to a selection of consultants. Shortly after my twenty-third birthday – and unusually – mother phoned me at work. Matthew had suddenly appeared and was coming to fetch me and so I was not to take the bus home. It was so utterly unexpected I couldn't think straight: a combination of excitement and nerves.

I walked out of the main entrance and there he was, sitting in his car waiting and watching.

He was on his way to Surrey to visit his mother, he explained, and had phoned to ask for a bed for the night. In the event, he stayed the weekend, came to my room at night when all was quiet, and that was the beginning of a passionate and painful love affair; a hopeless infatuation, a romantic ideal in my head, for I hardly knew him, so how could I love him? Yet, amazingly, it was Matthew who first spoke of love.

It was the Saturday of his May half term, He had come down from Staffordshire and we met at the National Gallery and then he took me out for lunch. At first, I felt awkward and shy. We had not seen each other for over six weeks and the letters that had been posted backwards and forwards contained the word games of barely hidden passion. Now, faced with his questioning eyes, I was terrified.

It was a hot, shimmering day and I wore a peacock-blue suit, a colour I thought set off the chestnut lights in my hair.

'You've cut your hair, 'he said. 'It's not too bad!' I couldn't finish my omelette; it stuck in my dry mouth.

'Don't you want anything more than an omelette?'

'I'm not hungry.'

He grinned knowingly, guessing why I had lost my appetite, but chemical excitement did not, I noticed, prevent him from thoroughly enjoying his meal.

'Eat up, 'he said. 'You don't want to lose any more weight. You're skinny enough already.'

After lunch, we walked back to his car and there we sat, oblivious to the passers-by. He was suddenly silent, but I sat chatting mindlessly. Suddenly he turned in a kind of desperation, put his arms round me and said, 'I think I'm in love with you.'

I can't tell you how I had longed for him to say that, but when he did, I only wanted to open the car door and escape. Instead, I managed to control my shyness enough to choke, 'Me too.'

'Oh, darling! Darling! Do you mean it?' His sudden outburst astonished me. It was like something out of the movies, corny and unreal.

'Yes.' I mumbled

'Kiss me, then. Kiss me properly.' And he pulled me to him, nearly crushing me, and I felt myself being absorbed by him; my lips, my tongue, my breasts tingled; my groin moved towards his hand. It was unexpected, spontaneous passion, which I mistook for love. I know now that it was infatuation, lust, call it whatever, but it wasn't love. Pete is the only man I have loved and when that happens, you know the difference.

So the affair was doomed to failure. He was now forty and wanting to take things very cautiously; I was twenty-three and in a rush to get married. I couldn't understand why there needed to be any delay; it hurt and angered me. And it was difficult, too, having to exist on letters only for long periods of time.

The next time he came to stay he was cooler, and stopped coming to my room at night. Frankly, I was utterly miserable, for I couldn't understand what was going on. All my love, it seemed, was not wanted and it had nowhere else to go but turn to fury. I wanted to hurt him as he was hurting me. I had to re-establish my self-esteem, some sort of dignity. I would not be put down; I would have the last word.

Today, I think what an idiot I was, but it's a long time ago and I was young. Now, alone and in trouble, I wished I could see him again. He would be an old man! I could tease him about that and I would have liked the opportunity to explain why I had written him such a cruel, childish letter to which of course he had responded with his usual quiet grace. He congratulated me on my sudden engagement to Peter and deeply regretted Mother's horrible cancer and promised to return all my letters as requested, if that was what I really wanted. I haven't seen him since. No chance to say sorry. No chance to just be friends. We could talk now. He would be a comfort and take me in his arms like a father and the pain would ease. I suspect that he was always a father figure; that that was part of the attraction. Always looking for a father.

That's what I wanted: a father to take all the pain away.

Chapter 10

It was cool and quiet in the entrance hall. A bee, caught behind the long panes of glass, buzzed frantically and I heard the intermittent tap, tap as its body hit the glass. Somewhere a clock struck three. The moment reminded me of childhood, when I had lain in bed with some ailment and listened to the silence of the afternoon, straining for the slightest human sound. Where had everybody gone? Now I only waited a second or two before Father Godfrey appeared, carrying a walking stick in one hand and a piece of paper in the other.

'I can push the brambles out of the way with this,' he said, waving the stick at me. 'We have far too many now. Anyway, come along and you can see for yourself.'

He opened the French windows, allowing me to go first.

'Now, let's see, where shall we start?' He looked around. 'I think the walled garden. Yes, the walled garden'

He led the way to the left, across the lawn and to the side of the house. We went through an old stone archway and into a square garden surrounded by high flint walls. The flower beds were planted with rose trees already in bloom and the warm air filled with their sweet perfume. Across each corner stood wooden seats, weathered greyish green.

'Well, this is the rose garden,' he announced, and I waited as he searched around for something else to say. Then, drawing breath, he continued, 'And as you can see it is not as well weeded as it should be.'

'It's still lovely, though.' Knowing I was nothing but a nuisance, taking up his time, but wanting to show appreciation, 'There's something magical about a walled garden. What is it, I wonder?'

'It's a good spot for the sun,' he murmured, 'and the brothers sometimes come here to sit and read or just to meditate.' He paused and cleared his throat slightly. There was something strong and regal about him. I thought he must have been very handsome once, but now his eyes were far away and weary and something in me wanted to put a hand on his arm to reassure him, comfort him.

'The trouble is,' – and he laughed – 'that whenever I come here to read, someone comes and wants to talk.' He thought for a moment. 'We don't get that much opportunity to talk here, and so...'

'That's very lovely,' I said, pointing to a pale-yellow rose on the wall beside us. 'Do you know what it's called?' I wanted to show interest and pleasure, for that would please him, I thought. I remember thinking that if I liked the garden then, surely, he would like me. Then I would exist. He shook his head. 'I'm afraid I'm no good at names. I appreciate flowers and gardens, but I've never studied it fully.' And he turned abruptly wanting to move on.

Once outside the garden, he stopped and, turning to me, said, 'Perhaps you would like to sit in the rose garden; it's very peaceful. You can come at more or less any time.'

'Oh lovely! I'll come tomorrow, perhaps.' My heart sank as I thought of tomorrow and the expanse of empty time.

But he was speaking again. 'We have some nice rhododendrons.' And he pointed to the path that led to the visitors' block. 'You know that part, of course. The blooms are particularly fine this year.' He touched a deep red bloom with the end of his stick. 'I don't quite know why. Well, we've had a very mild winter – perhaps that has something to do with it.'

I don't like rhododendrons. The leaves are too solid, too thick and shiny, too unbending and regular; for me the blooms are pompous and stiff, but I pretended they were lovely.

'We have some very colourful azaleas too.' He turned away from the path. 'But come this way.'

We were entering a long grassy avenue with huge overhanging beeches, which ran parallel to the house. It was cooler there as we walked in and out of the dark slabs of shadow. Every now and then, between the beeches, on either side and at irregular intervals, were the orange and pink azaleas that he had mentioned, and now he pointed them out by waving his stick to and fro.

'Very lovely, very lovely,' he muttered, almost to himself. 'This is the Monks' Walk,' he explained. 'I like to take a constitutional along here. I used to do it regularly when I first came, but I don't seem to have much time these days.' And then, 'Too much time indoors. It's not good.'

I imagined him striding along lonely paths on country walks, for he strode at such a pace that now I was almost running to keep up with him.

'Have you lived here a long time?'

'Fifty-three years. I came when I was twenty-nine. Now you know how old I am.' And he laughed like a schoolboy and strode out like someone impatient to cover a great distance quickly. 'Things have changed a lot.'

'In what way?'

He stopped. 'Well, we've got you, for a start! We didn't used to have women visitors, you know.' He gave me a cheerful glance. 'Oh! We've been dragged into the twentieth century all right. Never mind! Never mind! I'm sure it is all for the best.'

We continued walking. 'A funny thing happened once,' he said, changing the subject. 'I had a visitor and when he arrived I immediately brought him out here, thinking we could talk and have a good walk at the same time. It was only after we had been up and down here several times that he told me that he had walked from the station. And that is two miles away!' He laughed again. 'I think he must have been exhausted.' He moved ahead and muttered to himself, ' I never did that again.'

We carried on in silence and I wondered if he was trying to find some words for me about the children, about the accident. I thought perhaps that looking at the gardens was just an excuse to be alone so he could say something. But he said nothing and I found the silence awkward. I looked at the long grass and wished I could lie down in it.

'Who cuts all this grass?' I wasn't interested really.

'Oh, various of the brothers take it in turns. Nobody used to want to do it, but now we have one of those motor machines and they quite enjoy it. Of course, we used to employ several gardeners a long time ago, before the war. But the war stopped all that and now we can't afford to. We did employ a Polish gardener who wanted to learn English, but I'm afraid that with working alone in the gardens all day and taking silent meals, his English didn't improve at all!'

We both laughed.

'You have a garden I suppose?' he asked.

'Only a very small one. Now. We used to have a big one. It sloped down to the River Lee.' My mind went back to the elm trees and the cuckoo and the children laughing and playing and Dan messing about in the dinghy. But that was a different world, a secret world inside of me. A world no one could share. A lonely place.

'I expect you like gardening. Most women seem to.'

'I do, although I actually prefer growing vegetables.'

'Oh, well, let me show you our vegetable garden, then. We'll have to make a small detour.'

Peter had once planted onions between the flowers but he had planted them upside down and the shoots had turned yellow beneath the soil and the tiny white roots had shrivelled in the sun.

It always made a good story. He was no gardener!

'Oh! The doves. The doves have come.' He pointed to broken-down walls, which surrounded what had been the kitchen gardens, explaining that the walls were in need of repair and the doves pecked at the stonework, adding to the problem. 'So, if you don't mind, I'll just clap my hands and send them away.'

He clapped his hands hard and the smacks echoed round, bouncing off the walls, but the doves didn't stir. 'They won't go. No, they won't.' He stood and looked at them for a moment before shrugging his shoulders and turning away. 'Well, you can see it's not much of a place now, but we do still get a little fruit. I don't think there will be anything where we're going.'

'Where are, you going?'

'Wiltshire.' He waited and then added, 'I'm sure it will be very nice.'

'When exactly? You did mention something when I phoned.'

'Oh, we've only got three weeks left. You must forgive us if we're a bit upside down. We have such a lot of clearing out to do. It's been used by the order for seventy years. And the stuff we've collected…'

We were back in the avenue now and I was tired. But I'd decided that I would come back on my own and probably enjoy it.

Suddenly, there were the bells again, hollow and regular. He stopped where he was and gazed ahead.

'The Angelus,' he said. 'I'd forgotten the time. I'm afraid I'll have to show you the rest of the gardens tomorrow. I'll be late for evensong – and I'm giving the sermon too! Would you like to come to the chapel?' he asked, and then, suddenly remembering something, said, 'Oh, by the way, I found a copy of our ... well, I suppose you would call it a brochure or ... in-house rules.'

He grunted with some awkwardness and handed me the creased pamphlet, the paper he had been holding all this time. I took it and was grateful for the distraction from having to say no to the chapel. I was too nervous for that.

He turned. 'I must hurry. Can you find your own way back?' And then as an afterthought, 'Supper is at five-thirty, by the way.'

The sun had moved behind trees and the room was dark. I felt empty after the company of Father Godfrey. It's strange, but already home seemed somewhere that I had been separated from for a long time. Even the journey was a vague unreality. Had I really only been here for a few hours?

I lay back on the bed and lit a cigarette. A wasp kept diving between the edge of the curtain and the window. Its whirring body clipped spasmodically against the pane, the force sometimes knocking it onto the windowsill. It didn't understand that there was no way out. Hitting its head against a brick wall! How often had I been accused of doing just that? But now I couldn't imagine what could have been important enough. Getting the job, I wanted? Fighting to be loved by the wrong person? Getting Dan into the grammar school? How excited Fleur had been, fetching him on the first day. How smart he had looked in his new school uniform, and Fleur, too excited to wait for him to get out through the school gates, had run in to him through all the big boys, calling out to him in her high-pitched voice, and he had grabbed her hand with that shy smile of his. Fleur had started talking even before she reached him and I heard her above all the other voices.

The wasp was dancing on its back and I couldn't let that go on, so I slipped the pamphlet under its struggling body, opened the window and threw it out into the air. Through the open window, I could see behind the trees the wall of the rose garden.

Chapter 11

Before his sermon, Godfrey announced that, after supper, he would like to see anyone who was free to discuss arrangements for Monday when the man from Philips auction rooms was coming to see if they had anything worth selling. Probably all a waste of time, but one never knew. There were often stories of treasure worth millions found in attics.

He'd already decided to keep the Sunday sherry as it always was and had also thought of a possible answer to the Brother Joseph and rabbit problem. But he wasn't going to share his idea yet, although he thought he'd come up with a very satisfactory solution: that he would ask Brother Joseph to look after Rose Gregory. That would give him a sense of importance and help over the rabbit business, which he knew was going to be tricky. He didn't want to distress the man if he could help it.

At supper, he watched Rose without difficulty, for she kept her eyes on her food or looked straight ahead, as if she were gazing out of the windows. She ate a little more this time but still refused the jam tart and took an apple when Brother Oswald held out the fruit bowl for her. She had smiled momentarily and then turned away quickly. An impish face, he thought, with a mouth that quivered on the edge of a smile. Her complexion was pale beneath the brown hair, which was piled up, rather untidily. She didn't seem to go in for all that make-up stuff – not like some other women visitors, who looked more as if they were going to a bridge party than to chapel. Horrible. But this woman was different from the usual run. What was it? Something to do with anxiety , he couldn't remember exactly. He looked at her again, at the dark, defiant eyes, the haughty expression. No sign of anxiety that he could detect and he thought he knew anxiety when he saw it, but people tried to hide it in many ways. Something about her worried him. Was she safe to be here? He had enough to deal with already, without anything more. He was uneasy. Like the woman in his dreams, she was hidden from him.

He went straight to his room after supper. He'd said seven o'clock; that gave them time for a little recreation before the meeting. Brother Joseph should be along soon, though; he'd asked him to come as soon as he'd finished clearing up in the kitchen. Godfrey sat behind his desk. He always did that if he was conducting what he thought of as a more formal task, a trick he had learned from his father, who had had a senior post in the Indian civil service and once told him that when one was taking someone to task, one should conduct the interview from behind the desk, but at other times, when one wanted to appear conciliatory perhaps, then sitting in an armchair away from the desk was preferable.

His father had been an ambitious man and one who was continually disappointed, never quite reaching the heights of power for which he longed. He had gone out to India as a young man and lived there for the rest of his life, having married the daughter of a Swedish doctor, a deeply religious woman who had a tremendous influence over Godfrey, the only child of the marriage. There had always been conflict between his parents' ambitions for him: his father wanting him to follow him into the civil service, while his mother preferred the caring professions, medicine or teaching. In the event, he had pleased her by deciding to take holy orders, although she was rather dismayed when this eventually led to closed orders rather than the missionary world she had imagined. His father treated the whole matter with contempt once he had worn out his rages, and always blamed her for what he called her 'namby-pamby' ideas.

But I always tried so hard to please him, he thought. It was women who were his downfall. The European women terrified him with their overconfident and flirtatious manners. They were all-consuming and manipulative. Unfortunately, they found him attractive. No matter how he tried to draw away, distance himself or even, as he had on some occasions, be rude, the more they would only laugh and twist about and take hold of his arm saying, 'Oh! You're wicked!' He found them cloying and silly. His skin prickled still at the memory of one occasion when at a club dance he had gone outside to escape, finding a seat in the gardens away from all the noise and clamour. But someone followed him. Angela.

'Now, what are you doing out here all on your own?' And he felt her arms fold round his shoulders and her thick red lips nibble his ear. He had leapt up and she had laughed as he stood frozen with horror. She had grabbed him and pressed her hot, wet lips on his. He had flung her away like a snake and she had shrieked. For days afterwards he stayed indoors, mostly in his room. It had been something that he'd never been able to tell anyone and something that he didn't understand, except he knew he must be odd. 'Got a screw loose' – another of his father's expressions. All the other young men hung around the women, joking, flirting and later talking of their experiences, laughing amongst themselves. And the women were just as bad: making a play, using all their wiles, their eyes, their bodies. How he hated it!

With Padma it was different. Thank goodness for Padma, for she made him feel whole, and looking back after years of celibacy, he was especially grateful that she at least reassured him about his sexuality. He had spent so many very happy hours with her, made all the more special because of the secrecy. He often wondered what would have happened if his father had found out. He wished now, in his old age, that he had had the courage to confront him. Padma demanded nothing. Her eyes looked wide and cool and she listened. She walked quietly, serenely and spoke softly, like a child. They had walked in the gardens and along the lakeshores, sat and read from their respective books, and shared the mysteries of their religions. But although her father was an enlightened, well-educated man, one of the few Indians to work alongside the British in the civil service, they both knew that there was no question of their marrying. She went into an arranged marriage and he left for England and theological college. After a short period as a parish priest, he decided to enter closed orders, driven there by the adoration of his women parishioners.

He had thought, as a priest, he would be safe from the attentions of women. Nobody warned him about their infatuation with the cloth. But he soon learned, as he was besieged with supper invitations, presents of homemade cakes, books of poetry and religious stories. They gave up hours to clean the silver in the church, to work on fêtes. They attended every service, every meeting and squabbled amongst themselves with jealousy. He was entirely swamped and unable to extricate himself from the attention – and passion, when it came to Mrs Dearly. Under the guise of being safely married but in need of his help, she took up his last remaining hours, calling on him constantly for one reason or another and then, eventually, one night she suddenly threw herself at his feet said she loved him completely and then promptly asked his forgiveness and patience. He shuddered still, thinking about it. Anyway, it forced him to give up his work as a parish priest and to join the order. He had been in Burnham Abbey ever since.

Sometimes, in his middle years, he mourned the lack of a proper relationship and a family of his own. He had liked some women; Padma, he knew now, he had loved. He had never felt that way about a man, either. He had seen homosexual relationships, of course; they thrived under the guise of Christian love in all orders. He had seen too often the untold duplicity and complications of such friendships. It was going on under his nose right now. Oh yes! They might think no one knew. But he knew all right

There was an absurdly loud knock and immediately Brother Joseph put his head round the door, grinning like a naughty child. Godfrey was instantly irritated; it was impossible to deal with Joseph's ebullience. Why was he always so cheerful?

'Come in, Brother. You've finished clearing up, have you? Come and sit down.'

Brother Joseph produced an apple from his pocket and put it on the desk. 'I thought you might like this.' And Godfrey knew it was a peace offering in advance. 'Sorry about the fish,' Joseph gabbled. 'It was a bad batch Mr Williams brought. Late, too.' He paused for breath, his head nodding and his feet shuffling backwards and forwards on the spot as if he was wiping them on a doormat.

'Do sit down, Brother. Sit down. There are a few things I think we should speak about.'

Joseph pulled up the chair eagerly and so close he was leaning across the desk and staring into Godfrey's face. Godfrey tried to ignore the smell.

'Firstly, Brother,' he said avoiding Joseph's eyes,' I must remind you that the rabbit should not be in the kitchen. You must put it...' – he hesitated – 'somewhere else. Goodness knows what would happen if we ever had an inspection from the health and hygiene people.'

Joseph opened his mouth.

'And,' – Godfrey was not to be interrupted – 'your laundry needs more attention. I have asked you to be more careful about your clothes. It's a poor example for our younger members and dreadful for our visitors to see.'

Brother Joseph rolled the shiny green apple from one hand to the other and Godfrey could feel the irritation mounting.

'Brother, I know how much you enjoy being in the kitchen, but I think you've done your share of hard work there.'

Joseph blinked.

'As you say yourself,' – he hadn't, but Godfrey employed a familiar trick – 'it is limiting your time for personal matters: prayer, laundry and so forth, and in any case, there is something else that I would like you to do over the next few days. Of quite some value,' he added, as a bonus.

The apple halted in mid roll and Godfrey had an almost irresistible desire to snatch it off the table and stuff it into his top drawer. How could he ever have expected this child of a man to do anything properly? One had to feel pity for this gentle-natured innocent. One had to feel compassion.

Brother Joseph gave a little gasp and grinned hopefully.

'I am so very busy at the moment, Brother, but I do feel that we should find time for our visitor. She looks as if she would enjoy a bit of company. I took her round some of the grounds myself this afternoon and I do believe she enjoyed it. So perhaps you could just go along and make sure she has everything she needs. Oh, and that reminds me, check to see if she has a kettle and a tray with the usual tea things. Somehow I think we may have forgotten it this time.'

Before Godfrey could say another word, Joseph had squeezed himself up between the desk and the chair and was making for the door.'

'Joseph!' But the words 'Don't overdo it,' were lost on him as he hurried off towards the kitchen, mumbling happily to himself.

'God help us!' Godfrey sighed.

Chapter 12

The monks disappeared after supper just as they done after lunch, and once again I found myself alone in the corridor, but this time no one was waiting for me, so I made my way back across the lawn. Although I felt tired, it was such a gorgeous evening, the evening sun making everything yellowish, that I decided to go and sit for a few minutes in the rose garden.

It was mostly in shade then, for the sun was low and the walls cast great slabs of shadow across the paving and the beds, but one corner still held the sun and I went to sit there and enjoyed the dry, earthy smell of the evening and the sweetness of the roses, and recalled my childhood front garden.

It was a dull garden with its rectangle of neatly clipped grass surrounded by thick, high laurel hedges, but the flower beds outside the sitting-room window were full of roses in the summer.

My father was very proud of his roses and to please him I always smelled them and said how lovely they were. One Sunday afternoon he picked for me the yellow rose I had admired and put it in my bedroom as a surprise. He must have loved me very much.

He was my god on earth, my father. I was so proud of him. I thought his being a doctor was heroic. I still have this feeling about doctors to this day. He was a tall, potentially gangly man but somehow looked magnificent in his well-cut suits or Harris tweed jackets and grey flannels. He had an air about him, something strong, clever, wise. That's what I thought. I was always aware that his patients adored him and certainly he appeared to enjoy them more than his own family, who for some reason or another were a disappointment or an irritation to him. Often, I heard him making cutting remarks to Mother, who was frivolous and irresponsible, and he berated Duncan for being a fool of a son because he was hyperactive and a ragamuffin. However, this did not prevent him from spending what spare time he had playing with Duncan rather than me. I was simply permitted to watch the creation of complicated and ingenious Meccano cranes and pulleys, engines and bridges. Father and Duncan would kneel on the floor together, dead to rest of the world, as they worked on their inventions. And if I watched it had to be in silence; I was not allowed to distract them. There was the fabulous electric train set, too. I loved it, especially the stations and the little people with their suitcases and the guards with whistles and men with trolleys. There were horses and carts and railway bridges to cross. And the trains going underneath and round and about, with signals waving up and down. I was not allowed to touch but just to stand and watch. Yet occasionally I would dare to kneel beside them, longing for the very rare moment when father allowed me to 'have a go' working the trains. The excitement and the honour given to me was overwhelming, and my trains ran too fast and came off the rails and then I was sent away

So I found solace with my dolls. Here I created for myself the perfect family, the kind of family I wanted. I had three dolls and one I dressed as a boy – Johnnie; the girls were named Marguerite and Susan. I even had a husband, Roy, a sailor in the navy, who came home for holidays now and again. When I took my 'family' in the pram across the park, I would talk constantly to my children and husband, and sometimes Roy would be allowed to help push the pram, which meant I had to walk to one side and guide the pram with one hand only. More and more I withdrew into this private world where I could give and receive boundless love, and where I was needed and important. Loved. It compensated for the real world.

No doubt I was loved, but no one had much time for me. Mother preferred her friends and Father was too busy and very strict and I lived in fear of his disapproval. Poor Duncan had many beatings for his untidiness and clumsiness, and once I was once beaten with the back of a hairbrush.

I was standing in front of the bathroom mirror, trying to plait my hair. I hadn't done it on my own before and was getting in a real muddle, so I called Mother to come and help me, but she was in a hurry to go out somewhere and was annoyed, saying she really didn't have the time to spare. Nevertheless, she did begin to brush out my knots and mess, but so roughly and with such impatience that it really tugged and pulled at my scalp. It hurt me and I shouted out, 'Stop it, will you?' And Father overheard.

I was called to come at once to my room, where I was told to remove my knickers and to bend over. He beat me with the back of my hairbrush and I wet myself; the urine ran down my legs and into my socks. I never once hit Dan or Fleur. Not once.

But there were happy memories. On one occasion, Father took me with him in the car on his rounds and we went to visit an old lady who had an enormous lump on her face.

'She has a tumour on her face,' he said, 'so don't stare at it. Just talk to her nicely. She is very ill.' I went with him up the steep stairs of the cottage and into the darkened room, and stood beside him. In a great double bed with its brass bedstead, propped up against crumpled pillows, lay a shrivelled old lady, almost lost amongst the bedclothes. But she welcomed us with a smile and tapped the side of the bed with a frail hand, which hung limply from her wrist. Father sat on the side of the bed, but I stood, half hiding behind him, and stared hard at the top of the grey, wispy head in my struggle to keep my eyes off the horrible bulge in her face, so scared that I might have to go near her or even kiss her. She whispered something to Father and pointed towards her dressing table and Father carried back a box to her. She lifted her head with difficulty as she struggled to open it and in the end Father had to do it for her. Out of it she took a coral necklace, which she held out to me. Father nodded that I should take it and then said I was to go downstairs and wait for him in the garden.

I sat in long dry grass under an apple tree and tried to fit the necklace round my neck but it was too difficult and so I twisted it round my wrist and ran my fingers up and down the gritty pieces of dark pink coral and watched wasps swarming the juicy pulp of the fallen apples. Years later I gave the necklace to Fleur, and it is still in her box with all the other jewellery and 'precious ' stones that we collected together.

Mother was short and plumpish, with bright hazel eyes and a wickedly infectious laugh. She was intelligent, witty, vivacious and much too busy having a good time, playing tennis, bridge or going to tea parties. She didn't mean to be a bad wife and mother. But running a house was of no interest to her and although we had a cook and several housemaids, she was disorganised and untidy and the meals were often late because she had failed to give any instructions. Sometimes she forgot meals altogether. Behind the cushion in the morning room was years' worth of darning and mending. In desperation Father would sometimes sew on his own buttons. There were many arguments behind closed doors. And then 'Aunt' Prue offered to do some darning and mending. It was all a joke, of course; Mother was incorrigible, wasn't she? Father became increasingly irritated and bad tempered; he only ever laughed when 'Aunt' Pru was around. In the end, he sent Mother packing and married Pru.

At the time, I could find no fault with Mother. I loved her very much and quite accepted that she was 'far too busy' or 'exhausted' to do either this or that, and therefore I went out of my way to avoid troubling her.

My make-believe world was everything. I made up endless stories and little plays, which I so enjoyed acting out with my few friends. I especially remember one occasion when I arranged for a group of children, three girls and a boy, who was to play the role of prince, to come to my house after school. We would rehearse in the front garden so as not to get in the way and I asked them to bring their own tea in the form of sandwiches, because Mother was sure to be too busy to provide anything for them, and in any case I dreaded the huffing and puffing irritation of Mother whenever I asked her for anything. But when Mother saw us, and the children's jam sandwiches, curled and dry after a day at school, she looked momentarily ashamed and then turned her shame onto me.

'Fancy asking them to bring sandwiches! Really, Rose! What will their mothers think? You should have asked them to tea. Don't ever do anything like this again.' Then she disappeared and still didn't produce any tea for us, so it was just as well they had their sandwiches, dried up or not.

Yet later, some other time, not bedtime, because she never seemed to be around then, Mother said suddenly, kneeling on the floor and looking at me sadly, 'You don't have much of a life, do you?' and I hadn't understood at all. But a few days later she took me to see *Sixty Glorious Years* at the local cinema and that was one of the greatest moments of my childhood. I went home and dressed up in a long dress and put a veil over my head and looked in the mirror. Honestly, I'm telling you, I saw Queen Victoria looking back at me. 'Mummy, Mummy! Look! I look exactly the same, don't I?'

'Oh yes! Exactly!'

Dreaming again! But the gnats were worrying and I shook my head suddenly, shaking the memories away at the same time. I didn't want to think, and this sitting about with nothing to do was giving me time to think and the memories left me unsettled. I was detached from them and without any feelings, as if I was recalling some vague dream or story from a long-forgotten book. Sometime after the accident someone had said how angry I must feel, but I didn't. I had no energy for anger. But perhaps one day there would be an almighty explosion. Maybe I would explode or implode or something-plode. Something. Sometime.

I used to be only too capable of losing my temper and I do remember with great satisfaction the morning when I threw my cooked breakfast of fried bread and tomatoes on the floor in front of Mother and some guests who were staying, because she had promised me fried egg and had laughed secretly with her friends when I showed my disappointment. It was wonderful that rush of blind temper, so sudden, so uncontrolled. Where did it come from? I even surprised myself as I saw the red, oozing tomatoes squashed into the dining-room carpet and I can see their stupid, stunned faces even now. Mother didn't laugh then. I had power. I was powerful. I was someone to be reckoned with. My punishment was to go back to bed and miss breakfast altogether. But boy, was it worth it! How often I longed to do something like that again. Did it cross my mind that I would do something at the monastery? Of course not.

Chapter 13

I was waving the gnats away when I saw the monk with the rabbit coming through the arched wall. 'I've brought Francis to meet you,' he said as he puffed towards me 'It's after St Francis.'

It was greyish, wild rabbit with startling eyes, sniffing round my feet like a dog.

'That's very appropriate. The name.' I like rabbits and to show him I did I stroked it and it put its head up as if to catch the tips of my fingers. 'He's very tame, isn't he?' I was aware of the man's pale pupils staring at me through watery films, first grinning up at me and then down at his pet.

'And what's your name? Mine's Rose.'

'Joseph.'

'Brother Joseph?'

He nodded briefly. 'He thinks he's human.' And he bent twiddling his fingers on the rabbit's nose. 'Don't you! Don't you!'

He was a grubby, ill-shaven old man, now totally absorbed by his pet, and I, for all my revulsion, was touched by his fondness for this animal. 'How long have you had him?'

'The cat brought him in. I fed him with a bottle. He was only this big.' And he indicated a tiny ball with his hands. He had long curved, yellowish fingernails, not unlike the rabbit's claws I thought.

'The cat brought him in and he hopped behind the fridge. But he came out to me. With a carrot! It was Easter Saturday, so that's when he has his birthday. He got a new collar this year, didn't you, Francis? He hasn't got used to the collar yet. Keeps shaking his head all the time. But he's better today. His lead was Billie's. We love that lead, don't we?' He bent down and picked the rabbit up.

'Billie? Who's Billie?' His head dropped. I must have said something wrong.

Then, 'My best friend. Kept dogs. Over there.' He waved an arm. 'His leads are in the shed. He probably left them for me.' He shook his head backwards and forwards.

'I had a rabbit once,' I said, changing the subject, 'a white one with pink eyes.' But I don't think he heard me.

The rabbit put its paws up on his shoulder, its eyes bulging and nose quivering, yet perfectly at home. 'You can hold him if you like. He's used to it. I've had him since a baby. He sleeps with me. Not supposed to.' And he chuckled, peering at me, sort of asking me if I disapproved.

'I won't take him at the moment, if you don't mind.' But I did stroke him as he lay in his arms.

'I've just taken you a kettle,' he said. 'You can make a drink now. Brother Andrew is in charge of night drinks, but I like to make my own. His is too strong for me. We like to see to ourselves, don't we Francis?' He put the rabbit down and it leapt forward, jolting suddenly to a halt as the lead tightened, then twisted back on itself and panicked as it caught the lead in its back legs. The little monk unravelled the lead, his face reddening with the bending.

'I'll show you how to work it.' He turned back towards the archway.

Really, I had wanted to spend longer in the rose garden, but I followed behind the hopping rabbit. The light was fading fast now and it was probably time to be going, but I kind of dreaded being alone there.

'I thought I'd find you,' he said as he padded along the path towards my room. 'Father said he'd shown you round.' His head shook and I could see spittle in the corners of his mouth.

'I don't want to leave here. I shall be leaving all my friends behind.'

'Oh! Why? Are some people staying, then? 'He stopped and pointed away across the gardens beyond the long walk, a part I hadn't been to. 'They're over there. My friends!' and there was a slight glug in his throat as if he had choked on something. I hadn't, of course, the faintest idea what he was talking about and I didn't ask him because he suddenly seemed sad and I sensed that, like me, he couldn't explain to anyone else his own reality that, like me, he lived in a world of his own, a world that would not really make sense to anyone else. He was a child and I couldn't help wondering how he came to be here in the first place. Perhaps he hadn't always been this way. In a strange way, I wanted to protect him.

We arrived at my room and he opened the door quite unselfconsciously and went in. He pattered over to the chest of drawers, on which stood a tray with a kettle and tea things. He took up the kettle and turned to leave the room. 'Hold him,' he muttered, pushing the lead into my hands. 'The water's in there,' and he pointed towards the bathroom and then disappeared.

In the short time that he was getting the water, the rabbit managed to sprinkle the floor with small brown 'currants' and I wondered if he was nervous in the room with me. Joseph came back with water dripping from the kettle and dark patches soaking his black habit. He was in such a hurry!

'This is where you plug it in.'

'Yes, thanks. I'll be able to do that OK.'

'Do you want to make yourself a cup of tea now?' His eager face said it all.

'Would you like one? Come on, let's have one, shall we?'

He hitched the end of the lead over the doorknob and before I could do anything was opening the tin of teabags. 'I think there's enough teabags. I don't take sugar.' And he chuckled in his throat. 'I expect Francis would like a drop of milk. He usually does.' He took the cling film off the milk jug, poured some milk into the saucer, put it on the floor in front of the rabbit and stood watching while he sniffed at it. But the milk remained untouched. 'He doesn't want it. No, he doesn't.' He turned to me suddenly. 'Have you got animals?'

'Not at the moment.'

'That's a shame!'

He sat on the chair; I sat on the bed and watched as he drank some tea.

'How long have you lived here, Joseph? Is it OK to call you just Joseph?' He didn't answer; his mind was somewhere else.

'I always wanted a dog, but they weren't allowed. They didn't allow pets. We found a mouse once and Billie tried to keep it in a drawer, but Brother Anthony found out. He didn't half get into trouble.' He shook his head as he remembered.

I thought, He must mean some sort of boarding school. 'Did you go to a boarding school, then?'

He spoke between gulps of tea. 'Boys' home. St Dominic's. In Ireland. I'm Irish!' And he bent double with laughter, spilling tea. Some dribbled down his chin and onto his habit. When he'd finished, he got up without a word, as if he had forgotten I was there, put the cup down on the chest of drawers and, gently tugging the rabbit, left the room, shutting the door behind him.

I sat looking at the closed door and wished I could be like that, like someone who, having been given a cup of tea, could just walk out without a thank you or a goodbye or a word. Just go. But obviously, Joseph didn't care what I thought of him. It must be wonderful to be like that! Never to care what anyone thought.

It was not yet quite dark and a cloud of gnats hung in the air outside the window in the purple light. It was humid, for the breeze had dropped, and I hoped there would be a thunderstorm. I love storms and heavy rain and wind. I had always been able to get the children to sleep by telling them that it was raining. 'Listen to the great drops on the trees and curl up like a little bird in your nest, all snug and warm, and listen to the tap, tap, tap of the rain.' They loved that, and even if they didn't quite believe me, it was all right, because they wanted it to be so and they would giggle and curl up round their pillows and go to sleep. It was a trick I taught myself at boarding school, as sleep was my only escape from homesickness.

I loved my day school, would not miss a minute of it. Even when I was unwell, nothing would keep me at home. In my memory, every day was either hot sun or cold with a crisp, sharp frost. My legs would be covered in goose pimples and sting in the bitter air, but I didn't mind at all. It was always exciting and I was full of energy, running everywhere, never walking. I was bright at that school, always being praised and being awarded 'the top desk' to sit at. I was happy there. Boarding school was quite different.

Chapter 14

Duncan went to his first prep school when he was seven. Doesn't that seem dreadfully young? The house was suddenly tidy and quiet and Mother was very upset. I had never seen her like that before and someone told me to be very good because Mother was sad that Duncan had gone away. My being there didn't seem to cheer her up. Ah well! Instead, I heard the story of his going, heard it several times, as grown-ups were delighted by my brother's charming audacity. He had run off to join some boys playing football without even saying goodbye! All the grown-ups had marvelled and laughed at that so, when at the age of nine my turn came, I tried to do the same.

I didn't actually know where I was going; no one had taken me to see my new school nor told me anything about it. I only knew I was going to a new school because I was measured for the brown tweed school uniform. So, when my turn came to say goodbye, apprehensive and afraid as I was, I made a great fuss of rushing at them with overexcited goodbyes and then had dashed away, so that they should think me marvellous and brave as well.

It had been the most terrible hell. I had felt terrified and abandoned while the other girls seemed perfectly composed and self-assured. I disguised my fears by presenting to the world a noisy, brash confidence. I was perpetually joking and chatty and soon discovered I could make people laugh with my clowning about. It was a role I found difficult to drop. But at night, when everything had to be silent and when no one could see me, I would bite my pillow to deaden my crying. I am sure things would have been very different for me if I had received some letters or parcels from home.

All the other girls had daily post of tuck, warm gloves, a special pen, five shillings from an uncle, but nothing came for me. I didn't know, of course, that Mother and Father were in the process of separating and had no time nor emotions left to think about me. All I knew was that I had no visits, stayed alone in the common room while the others were taken out for tea at the weekends and spent hours in the lavatory when the others read their letters, because I couldn't bear the disgrace of having none myself. Having no visits, no letters meant you were an unpopular girl.

One day, after another post with nothing for me, I sat alone at a table in the common room and wrote a begging letter, forcing teardrops onto the letter so that the ink smudged, to make sure Mother could see how sad I was. 'I am so unhappy. I am crying. Please come and get me. I want to come home.' I felt so sure then that Mother would come at once to see me, and then everything would be all right

Letters home were posted by the housemistresses, Miss McFarlan and her friend Miss Scott-Davies and I, almost mad with anxiety and fearful that somehow they might forget to post my letter, kept pestering them, kept asking, 'Have you posted my letter yet?'

Several days went by and nothing was said, and so I asked again if they had posted the letter. 'It's very important,' I said.

Miss McFarlan, a tall, angular woman who wore brown socks, called me into their study, where Miss Scott-Davies was waiting, obviously expecting me, I could tell. Children are not stupid, you know. They understand a lot more than they can put into words. They have a kind of sixth sense. I did then. I knew this interview was not going to be good. I stood in front of them and waited. Then to my sickening horror my letter was produced. Miss McFarlan held it in her hand. 'Is the letter you were asking about?'

'Yes.'

'Well, I think we had better have a look at it, don't you, as it seems so important?'

'But it's only a letter to Mummy. It's just something I want her to know.'

'Open the letter and read it to us, please.'

What could I do? I couldn't refuse. Was too frightened. Of course, I now know that they had no right to demand such a thing and that I would have been within my rights to refuse. I wish I had said, 'That's my property. Please return it.' Or something like that. I'm so angry still. But I was only ten years old and away from home and scared. I had to do what they said. There was nothing else I could do. I was shaking as I opened my letter. And ashamed.

'Read it out please, Rose. A little louder please, Rose.'

I know my head was bent down. You don't forget these things.

Darling Mummy and Daddy

I am very unhappy here. I am crying all the time and I can't stop. At night, it is bad. Please, please come and get me. All the others get letters. Please, please will you just come to see me.

Your loving daughter
Rose

P.S. I am very, very homesick.

They sat dull-faced and listened to my humiliation.

'Well, I don't think we want Mummy to get letters like that, do you? We don't want Mummy to worry when there is nothing to worry about, so I think you should just tear the letter up. Go along!

Tear it up at once.'

I tore it up.

'In the basket, please.'

I threw the pieces of torn letter into the basket they indicated and with it threw away all hope.

I went back to the common room in a kind of broken despair and in my agitation knocked into a girl who was carrying an opened bottle of ink. The ink spilled on the floor and no amount of apologising and wiping up seemed to eradicate the crime, and so the big girls, the twelve-year-olds, decided there must be a court case; I was to be judged.

'We want Rose. We want Rose,' they chanted round and round the house and there was whispering and preparations. This was something I had to escape from. Like a wild animal running for its life, I ran to Miss Scott-Davies complaining of a stomach pain and begging could I please lie down in the sickroom. I hated the sickroom; it was the punishment room for children who talked after lights and once or twice I was told to go there. It was cold and dark and the bed was unmade and you stayed there all alone until morning. But now the sickroom was my only hope and, luckily, Miss Scott-Davies believed me, probably because I must have looked pretty unwell, and so I went and hid, but the girls knew where I was and they whispered outside the door and chanted again and again, 'We want Rose. We want Rose,' as they marched up and down outside the door.

And that was the moment I knew, finally, the truth: that I was unlovable because everyone hated me. From then on, I became constantly afraid of the next plot against me. And quite powerless to change anything. Powerless.

Often I imagined punishing, hurting, shutting-up for ever the people who made me suffer so. The bullies. I can't stand bullies. And that's the point really; that's why I did what I did my last night at the abbey. I'm sure of that. But then, as a child at school, I was too frightened to do anything, to stand up for myself, to show my anger. I just went on being afraid. But not any longer.

Anyhow, luckily, something came to my aid; I started to get real pains and in the end was rushed one night to a small, private hospital, where Father waited. Without any time to talk I was put to sleep and when I woke Mother was there. I asked her what had happened.

'You've had your appendix out.'

Oh, what a blessed relief it was to find myself away from school and Mother there too. Would they all be sorry now that I was ill? For what they did? In fact, I did receive a pile of letters from all the girls in the house. Friendly letters, funny letters, letters with drawings and jokes, and they all wrote how much they were looking forward to seeing me next term and they all ended with lots and loads and tons of love and kisses. I didn't believe a word of it. I could just see Miss McFarlan standing over them during prep and then checking the letters before they went out.

Mother sat with me most days, sitting so quietly, looking so thoughtful and sad; she was completely different, and I assumed that this was because I was ill. I was wrong. Soon I learned the truth, for during one of her long and silent visits she told me, when I was nearly better, that we would be moving near London as soon as I was well enough.

'Are we all going?' But I sensed, like a wild animal senses danger, that we would not all be going. We would be leaving Father behind.

'Who will look after Father?' And I started to cry, but Mother became extremely agitated in a way I had never seen before.

'Shush! Don't make a fuss. Father will be cross. You mustn't cry. Crying won't make any difference. Stop crying, Rose.' And so I didn't make any kind of fuss – not ever. And I don't cry, either.

At night, I worried and planned how I could stop this almighty catastrophe, how I could make everyone love each other again. I would run away; I would hide when the day to go came and that would stop it. But, of course, I did none of these things. I was a child in an adults' world and I was powerless. I imagined how I could change things, how I could exert my will, but in the real world I hid my feelings because people were cross otherwise. Nobody talked to me but spoke in whispers behind closed doors. And Mother cried. Mother cried a lot behind closed doors and I heard her. I'd never heard an adult cry before.

I was at home from the hospital only two days before Father drove us – and my white rabbit, Bambi, who was shut in the boot of the car – up to Middlesex. I was worried about Bambi being in the boot, but Father told me not to be silly; he was a tame rabbit and used to being shut up, he explained to me. And I was grateful for that, for he had not spoken to me for a long time. I've had a thing about caged animals ever since. Especially rabbits.

We drove in silence all the way. I tried one or two bright remarks, 'Oh! Look, aren't those trees lovely.' But there was no response and so I gave up and fell asleep. I fell asleep a lot after we moved.

When we arrived at the dismal little semi standing in a crescent of identical semis, my grey nothingness was immediately brightened by the sight of my grandmother, who had been sent on ahead, and was there with my uncle to greet us. Gran had always been there for me like nobody else, and I knew she loved me very much and I loved her to bits. Climbing into bed with her in the early hours of the morning was one of the loveliest things. She was a storybook Gran: warm, cuddly, singing songs and telling stories. 'I could eat you,' Gran would say, but now her grim expression confirmed my black foreboding that something catastrophic was happening. And Uncle John was there too.

Father took in the cases and the rabbit and left without a word. That was that. I ran after him, but the door shut behind him before I could get to him and then someone took my hand and told me to be good and quiet because Mother was not feeling very well. I knew Mother was not ill but sad. I remembered the crying from the night before and understood only too well the emptiness and despair she must have felt, and I couldn't bear it and so, after a short sleep on the unfamiliar, cold sofa, I set about to please her, trying to make her happy again.

First I put on the kettle to make everyone a cup of tea. I did a lot of singing and found an old cloth in the kitchen drawer and began to clean the morning-room windows. Mother was sitting at the table, her chin in her hands. I did a tap dance for her and someone said not to strain myself after my operation, but I took no notice. I had to bring life back somehow.

It was so much more family when Duncan came back from his school. But I can't remember what he did. For me, it was a grey, dull Christmas and I spent most of my time playing 'offices', sitting at the utilitarian, light oak table where the telephone stood. I wasn't interested in playing mothers and fathers any more. No more dolls. Somehow dolls seemed silly.

I reached over the bed for my cigarettes and the cheap lighter I had bought from the newsagents the day before. Was it really only yesterday? I lit the cigarette and stared at the dark trees and wondered about going over to Father Godfrey, knocking on his door. 'I've come for a chat. I've come to be put it right. There are a few questions I would like to ask you. Why am I having these strange mental blocks? Forgetting how to spell, forgetting my words, getting muddled with money? Can you help me, please? It's like a kind of dementia. A nightmare, you see.'

Chapter 15

Brother Joseph hummed tunelessly as he poured milk into the rabbit's blue and white bowl, which he kept under the sink amongst crumpled rags, a yellow plastic bucket and tin dustpan with balding brush. The rabbit was hopping about the kitchen, snuffling up crumbs and vegetable droppings left after the day's cooking. Joseph eyed him and shook his head. 'You're not supposed to be here, you know. Brother Bertram will grumble again. Grumble, grumble, isn't it?' With his toe, he pushed a curling piece of cabbage towards him. 'We're not going to be in here any more, Francis. What do you think about that? In the kitchen.'

His watery eyes stared into space and he straightened himself slightly, as if preparing for battle, while tutting warningly to his pet. But his tone changed to the familiar singsong, 'Here! Here! Here!' as he placed the saucer of milk down, shaking white drops onto the floor, which he smudged away with his foot. Again, the rabbit nosed at the milk, stopping every now and again, ears soft-back and eyes goggling. Joseph grinned as he watched him. 'You'll not be doing any harm. No, you won't. Look at you now!' And nodding cheerfully, he picked up the milk bottle and returned it to the bulky, old-fashioned fridge, before shuffling across to the larder, from which he took two carrots that lay amongst potatoes and onions in a broken wicker basket.

'Take them while I can,' he mumbled, pushing the carrots into one of his pockets. The rabbit havd returned to his exploration of the kitchen dirt. Joseph, suddenly fearful that one of the brothers might come in and find him, although it was past lights out, put the saucer, unwashed, into the cupboard and, clucking quietly to the rabbit, crept towards him and put his foot on the red lead,which lay on the floor.

He groaned with the effort of lifting Francis and stopped for a moment, breathless, before nudging his nose into the rabbit's fur. Then he tucked him under one arm and lifted his habit with his free hand so that he could climb the back stairs, which lead from the kitchen.

Sometimes, he tripped and it made a noise and he was always frightened that they would take the rabbit away. 'Shsh!' he whispered. 'Bertram will hear. Be good now! Be still, will you! It'll be outside with you. It will. It will.' But the animal wriggled violently as Joseph, breathing heavily, struggled up the stairs.

At the top, he released his habit and, taking his pet in both arms, shushed him to be still. Someone coughed behind a closed door and Joseph stood for a moment, under the dim hanging light, listening and catching his breath. There was a single light showing under the door at the end of the corridor. Brother Bertram must be reading, he thought, but by the time he had reached his door, the second on the right, the light went out soundlessly.

His room was smoky blue, dim and shadowy but he didn't switch on the light for he could see well enough to put the rabbit into the tall-sided cardboard box that stood at the foot of his bed. The rabbit twisted about in the flattened straw and an acrid smell of urine and dried droppings rose with the straw dust. Joseph closed his door quickly; the brothers were always complaining of the smell that emanated from his room. But to Joseph the smell was a comfort, reminding him of his childhood and St Dominic's.

There had been a smell about that old house, damp and powdery, acidy and sour, sometimes smelling of rotten fruit. He had been quite content there, as long as they were kind, not too cross. As long as Billie was there, nothing else much mattered. The only thing was that Billie, who slept in the bed next to his, cried at night. It was always after Brother Paul came for him. Especially chosen by Brother Paul. Joseph never understood. But he lay in his bed listening to the sobbing and it made him cry, too. He could hardly bear it. One night he crept from his bed and went to comfort him.

Sometimes other boys were the chosen ones at night. Did they cry too? All he knew was that he, Joseph, was never one of the chosen ones. And he was sorry about that, because you must be very special to be chosen, especially by Brother Paul.

'Billie would have loved you,' he muttered to the rabbit, then turned to the windows and drew the curtains halfway across. He took off his habit, pulling it awkwardly over his head, folded it, creased and grubby though it was, and placed it with utmost reverence over his chair, patting it and straightening it into position much as he would the altar cloth.

As usual, he kept on his slippers and grey socks while he said his prayers and now, still in his short-sleeved vest, which hung unbuttoned from his scraggy neck, and his long johns, he knelt by the bed like a child. He knew all the prayers by heart, just as he knew from memory the Gospels, the Prayer Book and any number of psalms. It was this uncanny ability to memorise that won him the attention of the father at St Dominic's who one memorable day suggested that he, Joseph, might like to serve at the Holy Communion, which he took daily. It was the most glorious moment. He was chosen at last.

Now he bent over his crumpled bedclothes and said his prayers. He pressed his hands into his eyes and heard the rabbit restless in his box. 'God, bless you, Francis.' God, he knew, wouldn't mind him being in the bedroom. He twisted his head and stared, through the gloom, at the box. The rabbit was still now and Joseph, feeling suddenly alone, gave way to his sorrow momentarily.

But not for long, for Joseph, as he often did at such times, screwed up his eyes and thought himself into the picture. He could see so clearly the Holy Mother standing beneath a great tree, and she was smiling. She was holding a baby in her arms and there was a pale, golden light shining through the trees onto the mother and child. Then he saw her standing at the high altar, dressed in black, her arms held up towards the stained-glass window where Jesus hung on the cross, his head lolling forward, his mouth screaming and the blood trickling down. And Mary wept. Finally, Joseph saw the engulfing white light, out of which walked the mother and son, and they were smiling. It was at this point that Joseph tried to go to them, tried to put himself into the picture, but he never could. He never could see the smile on his own face as he came to them. Joseph loved her smiling face, happy now, for he understood the pain she must have felt as she stood by the cross. He had felt like that when Billie died and he only began to feel the joy of Mary's smile after Francis came.

Now he said the *Gloria*, crossed himself and pushed himself up off his knees. He took one last look at the rabbit, gently removing a stick of straw that was stuck on his back, before removing his slippers and socks. Once in bed he wriggled onto his side and, putting his arm round his pillow, pulled it down and over his head so that he was almost completely hidden. He thought happily of the morning, for he was looking forward to fetching the lady visitor to Holy Communion. He loved it when they had visitors and he was proud to be looking after this one.

Chapter 16

I had to lie as flat as possible in the bath in order to soak myself, because the slightly rusty geyser only dribbled a few inches of hot water. I lay with the warm flannel over my top half to keep me warm and stared at the brown stain above the taps made by the drops of water that leaked from the geyser. It reminded me of tree bark. I lifted my leg to touch its rough outline with my toe and remembered the cedar cone Seamus had sent me. He had polished it to a gleaming chestnut glow and said it was the colour of my eyes. Romance! I have it still, in the jewellery box. Seamus was one of those unexpected things.

I hadn't wanted to go out for the day. My own holiday plans had collapsed without warning when my friend Mary phoned to say her father wouldn't let her go with me to France as we had planned. He thought we were too young, at eighteen, to go unaccompanied. I was so disappointed and fed-up; all I wanted was to be left alone. But for once Mother was really sympathetic, seemed to appreciate my disappointment and insisted that I went with her to take Duncan down to Bournemouth, where he was to stay with a school friend and his family. I really needed a lot of persuading, but I knew she was right. Hanging around at home on my own would have done nothing to improve my filthy mood.

The sight of the sea excited me, and I managed a cheerful face when introduced to the family. Seamus was not there, just his mother, father and sister, Molly. We sat in the faded lounge before lunch. His father, a vicar, was a surprisingly handsome man, his mother a tall, gawky, ungainly woman, whom I liked at once. Molly was relaxed and confident, gently browned by the sun and sea. They had already been there a week. She made me feel plain and dull, but I needn't have done, for she was friendly and kind.

Eventually, we went into lunch without Seamus, but he soon arrived, lean and tanned, and wearing a lugubrious expression. I had expected him to announce some dreadful news, but his face broke into the most radiant smile when he was introduced to me and he was transformed, all trace of his melancholy gone.

All through the meal, much to my shame, Mother recounted the woeful story of my failed holiday plans. It was almost as if she wanted everyone to feel sorry for me, but not in a nice way. She managed to make me feel pathetic.

Then from nowhere, Seamus's deep voice said, 'Well, stay with us.'

It took time for me to believe they really wanted me to stay and were not just sorry for me, and it was so uplifting when Molly, good-naturedly, argued that a female ally would be very welcome. They were, I knew at once, thoroughly nice people. So, that was it – I was to have a holiday after all.

We rushed to the shops, Mother and I, to buy the bare essentials: pyjamas, toothbrush, a change of pants and another top to go with the skirt I was wearing, another skirt and a bathing costume. Mother had never felt it necessary to spend much money on either me or Duncan, and so I was thrilled and excited by all this and grateful for what I saw then as her generosity.

Once alone with the family, Mother having returned home and Duncan no support to me, I know I was quiet and on my best behaviour, as all their attention was focused on me. Endless questions. Duncan was left to his own devices, having spent holidays with them before. He was perfectly at home. It never occurred to me then that me being there might spoil his holiday, and he never said. Seamus talked to me endlessly. He seemed to know so much, seemed clever and wise. His long, serious face would light up as he spoke and he laughed softly, darkly.

Sometimes Molly and I would be left alone on the beach while Seamus and Duncan did their own thing and then I lay in the heat, eyes closed and thinking all the time about Seamus. I didn't know what to do when Seamus teased me about my freckles or touched my back with wet seaweed.

Seamus managed things so well, allocating time carefully between Duncan and me; if anything, it was Molly who was left out, but she was several years older and happy to sunbathe and read and spend time with her parents, who never came down to the beach. To tell the truth, I'm not sure what they did all day long. I was only aware of Seamus. If Duncan was a bit fed up having to share his friend, he didn't show it, but then he often preferred to be alone, devising some complicated castle maze with sand or inventing crab traps.

On the last evening, we all went to the 'flicks', and not long into the film Seamus began tapping my hand and so, shy and unsure, I touched his fingertips. He took my hand, holding it firmly and quietly between both of his, as if to stop me from running away. His cool dry hands calmed my hot sticky ones.

On the way home, he sauntered with me more and more slowly so that Duncan and Molly were forced to go ahead without us and, halting in the shadows, he kissed me so seriously, so deliberately. 'I'll write, 'he said.

It was my first kiss. We were eighteen with all of life before us, and someone found me lovable. I was so happy. We wrote back and forth, newsy, loving letters. But then I made a huge mistake. I had an invitation to go up to Staffordshire to stay with the family. I hadn't seen Seamus since our week's holiday and was nervous.

Would he still like me? Would he still find me attractive? I forgot that on holiday I had no make-up or fancy clothes. I was just me. I should have thought, had the confidence. Instead I bought new clothes and even wore a hat to arrive in. My freckles were hidden by layers of make-up. He was there to meet me at the station and I knew at once that this me was not what he remembered or wanted. I knew at once. He was kind, as were all the family, but the spark had gone.

We have remained in touch by letter and the occasional phone call, but because life took us in different directions, to universities where we made new friends, the relationship never flourished. Yet I still feel a deep fondness for him, even after all these years. He liked me as I was: no make-up, no smart clothes. No showing off. No class clown. Just ordinary me. It was a tender, thoughtful friendship, which has lasted, not like the destructive passion I experienced with Matthew a few years later.

The bath water was cold. I lay still, fixed on the brown mark on the wall. Why was I remembering so much? I longed for Seamus. I longed for someone who had known and loved me when I was young and untouched. When I was alive. Would Father? No! Seamus was gentler and more fun. It hurts me to say so. I've never thought this way before. Perhaps that's what retreats to monasteries do for you. But just then, all because of that brown stain on the bathroom wall, I felt a yearning in the pit of my stomach.

Chapter 17

Brother Bertram stood by his door and listened. He was a flabby, bald-headed man with small eyes and thick lips. His pallid skin shone in the light and his podgy white hands fidgeted. He turned off his light quickly and quietly so that Joseph shouldn't know he was still up. But then Joseph was so stupid, seemed unaware of most things, most of the time. Bertram waited until he heard Joseph's door shut and then opened his just a fraction. He sniffed the air. And yes! The truth was that he could most definitely smell that disgusting rabbit smell coming from Joseph's room. Good, He could complain with impunity and he determined to go immediately to discuss the matter with the father abbot. As a senior member of the community it was permissible to go now, and in any case Godfrey wouldn't have the guts to refuse to see him. Bertram scoffed inwardly. How he despised the man! He would go now on the pretext that the abbot would be far too busy in the next few days. He had thought of a perfect reason for getting that stinking rabbit out of Joseph's room. He pulled on his habit over his pyjamas and quietly left his room, making his way in the opposite direction towards the main staircase, which led into the central lobby. He had told Oswald what he had planned to do, so they had cancelled their usual get-together.

Bertram had a smouldering grudge against Godfrey. Envy. Anger that Godfrey had been preferred as abbot before him, that he had not been appointed following Father Patrick's death, gnawed at him continuously. Bertram had worked so hard to be indispensable to Patrick and had felt sure that he would be the next in line, that Patrick would put his name forward as his successor. But no, Godfrey had been preferred, and Bertram thought Godfrey a weak, indecisive man.,Bertram saw his manner of conciliation and quiet patience as feeble incompetence, and was continually irritated by him. How often he had had to point out slackness and dereliction of duties to Godfrey. Nowadays the place was becoming more like a holiday camp than a religious institution. Brothers were slack in all sorts of ways. They talked in their rooms, were often late for prayers and he knew only too well the number of times they made little snacks for themselves in the kitchen. Quite against the rules. They lacked dedication to prayer and study. And now this ridiculous business of the rabbit. This slackness came down from the top, of course. As far as he was concerned, standards were going to the dogs. He would have taken the matter further if he thought it would do him any good. But he realised that no one was to be trusted, could be relied upon, except his Oswald, of course.

Brother Bertram was probably the only member of the community who was looking forward to the move, for he secretly hoped that there, in the new place and amongst new brethren, he could make a good impression and further his status at the same time. It was not impossible, even now, that he might be appointed abbot before he died. The fact was, he got things done. No one else, for example, could have managed to get Joseph removed from the kitchen; Godfrey would never have done so without being pushed. But Bertram had had the perfect argument: simply that Joseph's lack of hygiene was likely to cause illness sooner or later. That had been a clever move and Bertram was pleased with himself. Himself! It was a joke how easily he coud manipulate the Father.

What really angered Bertram was Joseph's manner, his irritatingly cheerful manner, quite inappropriate most of the time, and his utter refusal to recognise his own incompetence. He just went on through life undisturbed by anything. He was stupid, always smiling. Worst of all, though, was his lack of respect. That was insulting. The first time Bertram had tried to have Joseph removed from the kitchen Godfrey had argued strongly that Joseph needed something to be proud of, that he had always worked in the kitchen and loved so much to be in charge of the younger brothers, to know in advance what the menus were; the obvious pleasure it gave him to see them all 'tucking into the food'. That the kitchen was his world, his sole topic of conversation.

But Bertram had been clever; he was learning to handle – manipulate – the abbot rather well. So, he had nodded in agreement as the abbot spoke, shook his head with apparent sympathy, and appeared so concerned for the welfare of the obviously simple man who unfortunately couldn't be relied upon. It was he who had suggested that Mrs Gregory might need some 'looking after'. It was amusing how Godfrey listened to him. They didn't like each other, but Godfrey always listened.

Now he was going to manipulate Godfrey again; he had it all planned in his mind. It was like a combat, a game. And it was a game he was going to win. He, Bertram, was really the one with the power and he enjoyed it. It might not be easy, but he knew now how to plant ideas in Godfrey's mind yet allow him to think they were his own. That was most important! But he would separate Joseph from his rabbit if it was the last thing he did. He had become obsessed by the idea.

He moved carefully down the last few steps of the wide, highly polished staircase. There was only a dim greenish light emanating from a green bowl-shaped glass shade overhanging the hallway. Father Godfrey was always particular about turning off all unnecessary lights – reducing the electricity bill was one of the many ways in which they tried to lessen their costs – but his light was on, as Bertram knew it would be, for he always read late into the night, or so he claimed. Bertram hesitated before knocking. Was he about to make a fool of himself? Was it really necessary to see the old man at this time of night? Over a rabbit! He thought, He'll pretend he doesn't mind. He hasn't got the guts to tell me to go away. So it's his own fault for being so weak.

Bertram knocked on the door rather too firmly. It was a while, however, before Father Godfrey answered. Bertram was beginning to wish he hadn't gone, when all of a sudden the door opened.

'Ah! It's you.' He didn't seem surprised, but neither did he seem pleased.

'Just a word, Father, if you have a moment.'

'It's rather late, isn't it? But come in – just for a moment, then.'

Bertram was offered a chair facing the desk and Godfrey seated himself on the other side.

He's on the defensive, Bertram noted with some pleasure, and he assumed his seat slowly, deliberately before speaking.

'You know, of course, that Brother Joseph has that rabbit in his room?'

'I do. But we've already spoken about this.'

Bertram appeared to be thinking deeply. His look was one of concern. 'I really do think we should try to help Brother Joseph, Father. This animal must take him away from other duties: prayer, meditation, for example. It must very distracting for him.'

'I doubt whether he would see it like that, Brother.'

He's irritated, Bertram thought with some pleasure, and he's got that sulky,defensive look again. But Bertram would not be put off; it only made his assured victory all the sweeter.

Godfrey's's not taking me seriously, he thought, and his anger flushed around his neck. 'No! I'm sure he wouldn't, but then he doesn't yet know what the alternatives are, does he?'

Bertram himself smiled now to disguise his contempt. That silly, defensive look! But he wants to know. He'll listen.

Bertram had to be very careful now. 'I've given this a great deal of careful thought,' he articulated slowly.

'I'm sure you must have done.'

Bertram knew he must soften his approach. He leaned forward. 'What do you think we might do to house the animal? Kindly, of course. It surely can't be happy cooped up in a small box all night. Rabbits like to go out at night. Do their hunting for food and such like. It's surely not natural to be cooped up in a box indoors. Quite cruel really, if you think about it. What we do to wild creatures! And, of course, the room smells dreadfully, dreadfully. Quite awful. The smell permeates everywhere. The box is never cleaned out, you see. Of course, we all understand Brother Joseph's difficulties; he is not strong. It must be difficult for him.' He adopted his troubled expression, which had served him well in the past. 'The poor man needs our help, Father. Is there any way, do you think, we could help him to look after his pet better?'

Godfrey flicked the loose hair out of his eyes. 'I suppose you are thinking of the dog run.'

'What an excellent idea, Father. Of course, we would have to make them completely safe. Oh yes. We want brother Joseph to feel happy about the new arrangements, don't we? And, of course, it will be where his great friend kept the dogs. I'm sure that will please him.'

'I doubt that very much. Brother John's death and the grief … Well, I will put it to him. I do see that something has to be done.' His voice trailed away and he twisted in his chair, flicking at his hair again.

He's not happy, Bertram thought, without surprise

'I'll speak to him, but see to it that the run is made quite safe. And I mean quite safe, Brother. If you will.'

Chapter 18

Despite the bath, I couldn't sleep. I lay, eyes closed, trying to imagine the long grass with the dark tree above and listened for the movement of the leaves, but still I couldn't sleep. I tried to make my breathing regular and hypnotic – I'd read about that somewhere – but I could feel myself tensing and knew it was useless. It was like a first night back at school: the unfamiliar bed, hard and cold, and the covers flimsy and unprotective.

I must have been about six. It was a Sunday and I had gone down to breakfast as usual but was told I couldn't have anything to eat because I was going to have my tonsils out. I knew what that meant. I don't think I was frightened. I think I just accepted it. It's funny how grown-ups were always so secretive – nothing was ever discussed or explained. But then, perhaps it was better not to know in advance. If I had had time to think about it then, surely, I would have been a bit scared. Now, all of a sudden, I was to go to hospital with no preparation, no warning. I always talked to Dan and Fleur about everything. We had no secrets from each other.

My father drove me to a big house, took me to a small room and told me to undress. It seemed strange to be undressing in the middle of a Sunday morning, strange to be getting into the neatly starched, cold bed when I was feeling perfectly well. Some other people came into the room and Father gave me a small metal rod with rings running up and down it and told me to count the rings, slowly, out loud. Someone put a red rubber mask over my face and as I counted, my voice became louder, there was a peculiar buzzing in my ears and I spiralled away, out of control, helpless.

I woke up to find a nurse sitting on the bed and a hot sticky rubber sheet covering my chest. I could feel my mouth filling with warm, thick liquid, which I spat into the metal bowl the nurse held in front of me. I was frightened by the blood and I cannot tell you how painful my throat was, searing raw and burning. It was days before I could eat or drink. Years later when I was suffering continually with a lost voice, the specialist who looked at my throat said, 'My God, who on earth butchered you?'

I thought about all the times I had been in hospital. A tooth had to be cut out and the woman in the bed beside me had a blue rinse, which she told me she had done especially for coming into hospital. She always liked to look her best! To be sure, she didn't look ill, but then her face was immaculately and heavily made-up. She sat, propped against the pillows, wearing lacy bedjackets, a new one for every day of the week, and gave me a detailed account of her gallstones, which had now been removed and were sitting in a jar, which she rattled towards me victoriously.

I hate hospitals. I am scared of illness now, so I had Dan at home. He was a plump, bald-headed, placid baby with large, enquiring eyes. And Fleur, born six years later, was red, scrawny, with spikes of fine hair. Restless, demanding, determined. She used to lie on her back with one knee folded and her tiny hands behind her head. Dan grew up to be thoughtful, reliable and easy-going; Fleur never stopped talking, couldn't concentrate on anything for long and either loved or hated with ferocity. I knew I had a very special bond with Dan, but I loved Fleur beyond words. When exhausted, she would crawl into my lap and fall asleep. It was like sheltering a wild animal. It felt very special.

As Dan grew up he tried to hide his adoration for Fleur behind a facade of casual indifference, but he fooled no one, least of all Fleur, who was his shadow. Often at night we would find she had crawled into bed with him. She would wriggle and giggle and hide under the bedclothes. He would get no sleep while she was there and had to be removed kicking and giggling, 'Just one more cuddle!' Everything he played, she wanted to join in. At two years old, she would insist on playing 'Nopoly', and patiently Dan would give her a house to arrange or let her hand out the money. There were times, of course, when he did things without her; she couldn't always tag along, nor should she have done. On those occasions, I would have to find something to distract her. When Dan had a party, for instance, I arranged for Fleur to have one too, but in another part of the house, otherwise she would have been continually interfering.

What did they like to eat? This is one of the terrible things. I can't remember. I can remember general things like roasts and roast potatoes. They always wanted to eat one on the end of a fork before lunch. I could remember the early-morning cups of tea with iced diamond-shaped biscuits, but what in particular did they like? For Christ's sake, I can't remember. Tell me why can't I remember the precious, private little things that only a parent could know! It's all a blur. Everything is in generalities and I can't bear it.

And I can't ask Peter.

I got out of bed, lit a cigarette and opened the door. It was warm and clammy, and the chimneys and roof of the house appeared remote and aloof. I thought, I must be mad to stick myself in a place like this. And then, wryly, But that figures!

The tip of the cigarette glowed and caught the edges of the smoke. I shivered, despite the closeness of the night, and my stomach felt hollow and I decided that perhaps a cup of tea and a biscuit would send me to sleep.

Chapter 19

The rabbit, sensing dawn, started scrabbling about in the box, and Joseph opened his eyes and listened joyfully, comforted by the familiar sound. He never failed to feel the pleasurable anticipation of seeing his rabbit for the first time each day. He rolled out of bed immediately, his own scrabbling movements imitating the rabbit's as he pushed away the bedclothes with his legs. He greeted the rabbit with a 'Chuck! Chuck!' and ruffled his ears before padding down to the lavatory, dressed only in his vest and pants. Everywhere was silence; he was always the first up.

As it was Sunday and he was to serve at Mass, he ran the electric razor, a Christmas present from all the brothers, over his coarse stubble but without the least interest. He didn't trouble to look in the mirror that hung above the washbasin in his room, and when he had finished his face was dotted with clumps of whiskers that stuck out from his chin and cheeks, but he didn't notice as he hurriedly rinsed his hands under the cold water. Drying them on his pants, he dragged his habit over his head.

He moved quickly, excited like a child before Christmas. 'Come on, Francis,' he whispered, and fitted the red lead onto the rabbit's collar before lifting him out of the box. He tried shutting his bedroom door behind him with his elbow, but it was too difficult and so he left it open, with the damp, hot smell of rotting manure escaping behind him.

Once in the kitchen, he put the rabbit down on the floor while he opened the back door and then, holding onto the lead, he pulled the rabbit, dog-like, out into the garden. It was just light, so Joseph could see enough to find the long rope encircling the trunk of the cedar that stood in the middle of the lawn, and tied this and the lead together with a rough knot. Then he trotted back to the dustbins standing outside the door and found yesterday's vegetable peelings, which he had previously wrapped in newspaper, and these he dropped in front of the rabbit, who was already nibbling at yesterday's remains, still scattered untidily around the tree. The dirty paper Joseph stuffed in his pocket as he turned and shuffled his way back through the kitchen door.

It was dark in the chapel, but he found his way easily to the altar and felt for the box of matches, which he always hid from the others, behind one of the candlesticks. He shouldn't do this, he knew, but he enjoyed lighting the candles so much, and he wanted to make quite sure that if by any chance a brother should get to the chapel before him, then the brother, not being able to find the matches in the vestry, would not be able to light the candles before he arrived to do it. So he nodded with satisfaction as he took the box in his hand.

The tall, white candles were too high for him to reach and so, as usual, he had to stand on Father Godfrey's prayer stool. He pulled it over to the altar and with one hand on it for support, he stepped up awkwardly, his foot catching the hem of his habit. Once he had balanced himself, he struck a match, but with nodding head and shaking hand, he had difficulty in touching the wicks with the small flame. He was obliged to light several matches, which he dropped carelessly on the carpet, before finally succeeding in setting the candles alight.

The altar came alive in the flickering, yellow light and deep shadows wavered on the walls and floor. Joseph stepped down, tucked the matches back behind the candlestick again, pulled back the stool and then made his way to the vestry. From the cupboard he took out the silver plate and chalice, placing them first on a small wooden table beside the cupboard, before carefully and slowly counting out twelve round white wafers, which he placed delicately onto the dish. He managed to arrange the white discs in a circular pattern, every circle touching the next exactly. Then he poured the wine into the chalice, spilling two red drops onto the white cloth. He didn't appear to notice, but took first the chalice and then the plate, and put them carefully in the centre of the altar. He took a step backwards and stood admiring his work, then turning abruptly, hurried to the front pew. The paper in which he had wrapped the vegetable scraps crackled noisily in his pocket as he lowered himself onto his knees.

The low sunlight was filtering through the high windows now, lending the chapel the yellow glow of early morning, but Joseph, in his black habit and kneeling in the shadowy pew, could barely be seen. He pushed clenched fists into his eyes and prepared himself for Mass and thought about his sins; he knew he must have committed some since last Mass – he had been disobedient over Francis. It was wrong, he knew, to take him into the kitchen and to have him in his room, but somehow he couldn't feel the wrath of God. Bertram seemed to mind more than God. Still, he must try harder. And perhaps he had not read the Bible as much as he should, but he knew it off by heart anyway. And as for his prayers, well, the point was that he talked to God all the time anyway. He either talked to Francis or to God.

How amiable are thy tabernacles, O Lord of Hosts!
My soul longeth and fainteth for the courts of the Lord:
My heart and my flesh crieth out for the living God.
Yea, the sparrow hath found an house, and the swallow a nest for herself, where she may lay her young, even thine altars, O Lord of Hosts, my King and my God.
Blessed are they that dwell in thy house: they will be still praising thee.

Joseph looked up at the figure that hung on the wall above the altar. He thought of Jesus at the Last Supper and knew that the Lord would be there, as He had promised when he, Joseph, took the round white disc in his mouth and drank the wine from the silver chalice. It was, for him, the dearest thing in his life; that and Billie. 'Teach me to be your faithful soldier and servant,' he whispered and then remembered the visitor. Surely, she would want to come to Mass this morning. He must go and fetch her.

Chapter 20

I woke with such a start. The hammering seemed to come from somewhere across a river, a long way away. It took me several moments to realise where I was and that someone was knocking on my door. I leapt off the bed, black dots spinning dizzily. I know I called, 'Who is it?'

Someone shouted back, 'It's Mass soon,' and I recognised the high, quavering voice of the little monk with the rabbit. I unlocked the door and called out, 'When? When is it?' but he was already halfway down the path before he could answer me.

I had to sit down, still feeling peculiar after the dreaming and sudden waking. I wanted to make myself a cup of tea, but I knew I had no time and that now I had to pluck up the courage and go to morning Mass. How stupid is it that despite everything I cared how I would look? Can you believe that? But there was no time. My hair was a mess, so I just piled it up in a knot and pulled on the blue jeans and top I had been wearing the day before.

The low sun caught the edges of the tree trunks and lit up patches of grass and the tips of the rhododendron leaves. It was going to be another warm day but just then it was cool; the path was wet with dew and the early morning damp from the lawn, as I crossed it, spread dark stains on my sandals.

The French windows of the central lobby were slightly open

and I had the feeling that the little monk had deliberately left them open for me. I had no idea where I was supposed to go but guessed that it was somewhere beyond the dining room. I was desperate not to be late, wanting to go in unnoticed. Then, to my relief, I saw Father Godfrey crossing the hall. He was wearing a richly embroidered green and gold cape. 'Good morning,' he nodded and proceeded through the door that led to the dining room, and I followed with some uncertainty, feeling a surge of anger that nobody made anything clear to me.

But outside the chapel he stopped and indicated that I should go on in in front of him.

'Where shall I sit?'

'Oh, anywhere, anywhere at all.' And then added with the chuckle that was already familiar, 'We don't have special places any more.'

The gnome-like backs of the hooded brothers were barely lit by the flat, grey light of the early morning, which seeped through the nave windows, contrasting with the chancel's artificial yellow light, which flooded from a circle of bulbs housed by discoloured parchment shades.

I took a place quickly in the back row, far away from everyone else, and heard the cushioned strides of Father Godfrey as he passed me. Glancing up as he approached the altar, I saw the 'rabbit brother' who had woken me kneeling on the right, his palms together in prayer, his head nodding every so often. I wondered what his position was in the community. From what I'd seen so far, he appeared very much to be a law unto himself. I wondered about the rabbit. It was very unusual, to say the least. And then I questioned, Are they happy here? Are they kind to each other?

I stared at the Christ figure hanging on the cross, hypnotised by those outstretched arms. Outstretched arms should mean love, welcome, welcoming love. I wanted to cry out: 'Bollocks. It's all a load of bollocks.' And I felt the prickling of tears. One of the reasons

I didn't want to go to Mass was my fear of crying, of being seen to cry. I had been betrayed: those arms of welcome, of love, of help, were useless. 'I'm not the only one,' I thought for the thousandth time. Those arms – they had meant so much to me once. But when it came to it, when the moment came, they were powerless; I was powerless; I just kind of stood by and could do nothing. How could I have been so useless, helpless? Because there was no help. I was weighed down, drowning, sinking into the black pit of madness. That's how it felt and there have never been any words. It's pointless, you see. A waste of energy. It happened, and that is that.

It had been different once. Funny thing – I can still remember standing in the nursery and crying because it was the day Jesus was killed on the cross. Good Friday. I was very young, so how did I – the little girl who jumped off the dining-room table because she wanted to fly – know that? Perhaps through Granny, who had said simple prayers with me? Or, now I come to think of it, it was probably my friend, Margaret Cousins, who was very holy and took me to Sunday school. Yes, I think it must have been because of Margaret. I bet she became a nun; she was the type. But, of course, when we were moved away I lost all my friends and I never heard from her again.

I started going to church at boarding school. We walked in a crocodile down the hill to the huge cathedral. And school assemblies were religious occasions with readings, prayers and a sermon. Once a week Canon Rogers came and took the school service, his head and body jerking uncontrollably and the girls would titter and nudge each other. I was embarrassed for him; I couldn't bear to look. All I knew was that he was very brave to stand up in front of a hall full of giggling, unsympathetic girls. It was partly for this reason that I asked to join his confirmation classes.

Then the heated debates began. Could you go to heaven without being a Christian? Was there really a life after death? Should you always turn the other cheek? What good did Jesus do by dying? I entered the debates with the fierce passion of a fervent twelve-year-old and was certain and unbending. Jesus could have prevented His own death had He wished. God could have intervened, for He did have the power to move mountains; you only needed faith. If you couldn't move a mountain, it was because you didn't have enough faith. It was as simple as that. Suffering brought you closer to God and if it didn't, then you couldn't have loved Him much in the first place. It all sounds so ridiculous now, but that's how I was, and during our sessions and Canon Rogers noticed me. Though I was inexperienced and rather too fiery, he was patient and I could tell he thought something of me. That was important to me then. Probably still is. Now what would he say to me, this speechless, prayerless woman? What would he say to the stubborn, tearless challenge: 'If You want me, You do something. I can do no more.'

Scilla, my best friend at school, and I went to confession in the vast cathedral on the Thursday evening before Confirmation Sunday. Everything was silent and waiting, and our footsteps echoed as we approached Canon Rogers, who had taken on an awesome presence as, dressed in long, rich clothes, he waited, solemn and still, in the little confessional room.

I was literally terrified; it was like going in to see God, not someone I knew. I went in trembling and knelt before him and took out the piece of paper on which were written all my sins. At least all the sins I could think of.

'Read them out to me.' He didn't seem like my friend any more.

My voice would hardly come out.

'Speak up.'

'I don't always love God as much as I should. Sometimes I'm unkind to other girls. I have a bad temper and I'm noisy. Sometimes I tell lies. I speak without thinking. I'm selfish. I'm rude to my mother. My mind wanders when I'm in church and when I say my prayers. I am proud. I have stolen things.' Then I stopped because my mouth was dry.

'What have you stolen?'

'Sweets from my grandmother's sweet tin when she is not looking.'

'Oh, I see.' Did I detect a twinkle in his voice? I had my head bowed.

'And how are you unkind to other girls?'

'I follow the crowd when they are saying unkind things because I'm afraid. And I'm not friendly to people I don't like. I don't fix a church walk with a girl because she has really awful spots and it makes me feel sick.'

'Will you try to be stronger in these matters?'

'Yes, Father.'

'You have not strayed far have you, my child? God loves you and all your sins are forgiven you and the slate is clean.'

Oh, the relief. I knew I would cry from relief. From the kindness, for the forgiveness. He put both hands on my head.

'God have mercy upon you, pardon and deliver you from all your sins, confirm and strengthen you in all goodness, and bring you to life eternal, through Jesus Christ our Lord. Amen.'

I felt his hands on my head and then all I wanted to do was to escape. He was going to ask more of me than I could give. I knew it.

'Rose.'

'Yes.'

'You are God's child. Are you willing to give your life to Him?'

'Yes.'

'Always?'

'Yes. I will try'

'Good, Rose, and God bless you always. Now go and pray for a little while.'

I wanted to run from the room.

I walked back to school with Scilla, who went in after me. It was dark and windy that November evening. Neither of us spoke a word. I felt energised, happy. I could do anything now – except keep silent!

I whispered to Scilla, 'I daren't say anything. I'm frightened to open my mouth. I've never been so holy before and if I speak I'm sure to ruin everything.'

The monks were filing up for communion. Father Godfrey held up the silver chalice and Brother Joseph stood beside him holding out the plate. I didn't go up. I just watched the brothers go one by one, kneel at the chancel step and put their heads back to receive the sacraments. I watched, pitying their naivety as Father Godfrey took a wafer from the plate, which Brother Joseph held, dipped it into the cup and placed it into the open mouth. I could hear the mumbling every time he did so. I had been fascinated by that secretive mumbling before I'd understood what was going on and, even now, it seemed private and mysterious. Each monk crossed himself before standing and returning to his place.

Father Godfrey turned towards the altar, the service now concluding, but the little monk remained, facing us, waiting expectantly. I dropped my head, certain he was looking for me, expecting me to go up. Please don't make a fuss, I thought. But after a moment he, too, turned and placed the silver plate on the altar and then took up his kneeling position. I had disappointed him.

They all stood when Father Godfrey stood and the monks filed out behind him, but I stayed where I was. I sat, staring ahead, thinking I'd got to work things out. I'd got to get a grip on myself. But I didn't know what sort of grip. After all, to all intents and purposes, I had got a very good grip on things. I was living a perfectly normal life, doing perfectly normal things, like everyone else. After all, I wouldn't have been there except for the odd memory lapses. I tried testing my memory: phone numbers, titles of the books by my bed, films I had seen, theatres, but it was exhausting and unproductive.

'Mrs Gregory! Mrs Gregory!' I turned abruptly to see Brother Joseph leaning towards me. 'It's breakfast.'

He was serving at table and brought me cereal, a boiled egg, toast and a large cup of tea, slopped in the saucer. I smiled because he deserved a smile, I thought. Nobody took any notice: they were all too busy eating. A young brother, the one with the spotty face, mumbled from Luke's Gospel; again, nobody appeared to be listening. I noticed the way they launched into the food. Mouthfuls of tea were gulped to wash down even larger mouthfuls of cereal and toast. They bent their heads to the task, much as they had while praying. The twanging of the metal cutlery on the white china and the clanging of cups on saucers rang in a kind of rhythmic chorus.

He was there. The man I mentioned before; the one who was not a monk. He was there and raised his spoon to me in a quick greeting. And this time I nodded in reply. But that was all. I tried not to catch his eye again, concentrating on my boiled egg and then on the view from the windows.

The garden was already filled with sunlight, which threw armfuls of shadow as its rays blanched through the trees, and I suddenly longed to be outside, to go to the walled garden and to sit and look at the lights and shades, the tones of the garden. To smell the freshness, the sweetness, away from this stuffy claustrophobia. I wanted the warmth of the sun very badly indeed. Perhaps I would paint.

After breakfast, they all disappeared, as before. No one was in the hall this time, which was a kind of relief. I noticed the rabbit as I crossed the lawn and stood watching it for a moment. It was perfectly at home hopping around on the end of the rope. I went over to stroke it, remembering the white rabbit Father had bought me in place of the dog I had really wanted. This rabbit had a far better life than my poor Bambi, which had been cooped up in a small cage, generally thick with droppings and acidly wet with urine. Father had made a run, but the rabbit always managed to claw its way out and then we had the difficult task of catching it. In the end, it was seldom free. No, it had had an awful life. This Francis, though, seemed happy, free and fat. As I approached, it stopped eating, pricked its ears forward for a moment and then quickly hopped away until it was jerked to a halt by the end of the rope. 'All right, I'm not going to hurt you. I won't touch you if it frightens you.'

I didn't stay long, and after a moment of curiosity, the rabbit returned to the vegetable scraps.

Chapter 21

I stood, wondering what to do next; there was nothing but go back to my room. I drew back the curtains, straightened out the bedcovers, shoved a jumper and some underclothes into one of the drawers and hung up a skirt, a pair of trousers and a shirt in the curtained corner. Why did I bother to look at myself in the mirror? To see if I looked so washed out? But I wasn't as pale as before; that eased my anxiety, and I didn't care that my hair looked a mess. Nothing seemed important at that moment, but I rummaged in my toilet bag and found the tortoiseshell comb, which I pushed into a bundled-up knot on the top of my head. And then, of course, I would go to the walled garden for a smoke and take my book, in case anyone came along. At least I could make a pretence of reading.

The rose garden was empty and I chose the corner where the sun had reached and lit my cigarette. Wood pigeons echoed from somewhere, but there was no cuckoo. Nor any sound of water.

We had debated long and hard whether to buy the house with the river at the bottom of the garden. Was it too risky with a four-year-old? But it was such a welcoming old house, and as well as the river, I had fallen in love with the wooden veranda that ran along the back, despite its peeling paint and rotten floorboards. The house had no front garden, just a few steps and some iron railings down to the street, but the back was sprawling and wild with unpruned fruit trees that almost obscured the view of the river. There was one old pear tree and in August the grass was strewn with yellow, rotting pears, which attracted hordes of wasps. But what should we do about the river? Really it was no more than a large stream, for it was only roughly thirty feet across and shallow, three to four feet in depth at the most and in a drought we thought it could dry up altogether, although in fact it never did as long as we lived there. Like old Father Thames, it kept going, somehow. It was always clear and pebbly with weeds and reeds that needed clearing a bit every year, and then you could easily see the slippery brown fish as they glided nonchalantly above the stones. But a child could drown there. I was finally persuaded that it would be all right when Peter described the fence he would build, and the gate that we could safely padlock. Because the garden sloped down to the stream we could still see it over the fence, which was tall enough to deter a child.

The fence was in place before we moved in at the end of August, a week before Dan's fourth birthday, but even so we both watched him like hawks and if he disappeared behind the trees for more than a minute, one or other of us would run after him. In truth, it was safe and Dan was perfectly content to stand at the fence and look out. In fact, there were, then, far more interesting things to attract his attention in the new house and garden. The river seemed rather tame in comparison with the tree house Peter built with some of the timber left over from repairing the veranda, and the cellar, which could be approached by stone steps leading off the kitchen.

Our first job in the garden was to thin out the trees so that we could enjoy the river and the trees beyond from the house and the veranda. Neighbouring riverside houses had manicured lawns sweeping down to smart landing stages and well-varnished summer houses, but we kept the old wildness and Peter simply patched up the dilapidated landing stage. We bought an orange rubber dinghy to begin with. It was light and unsinkable, a good first boat for any child, and we both spent more time than we should have done either rowing Dan up to the bridge and the public landing stage from where we could walk within a few minutes to the shops, or we simply drifted downstream, trailing fishing nets or lines.

Dan quickly learned to row and all the codes of the river and so for his sixth birthday we bought him a small, light rowing boat. He was so sensible and reliable that we had no fears now for his safety. He developed into a fine fisherman, as Peter taught him how to use a rod and to bait the hooks with bread pellets or worms found in the garden. If he caught a fish he always put it in a bucket so that he could show us before throwing back. We all so enjoyed the river on sunny days when the pebbles glistened yellow and on rainy days when the drops bounced off the water. You could hear it at night; it was the loveliest sound in the world. We had to admit that it would have been nice to have a summer house by the river for cold and bright or rainy days, and Peter often discussed the design with me, but it never happened, of course.

Fleur was born in the November after Dan's sixth birthday but her pet name was Flower mostly, although like all families I suppose we called her many flower names as family fun. Come here, Buttercup, Lilly, Dandylion, Snowdrop, Daffodil, and she would laugh. But one day she stood with hands on hips and announced 'I want to be Flower.' but mostly when she was being particularly sweet, it was Flower. Dan called her Toadstool if she was being difficult and this made her giggle as well.

By the time she could crawl, Peter had fixed wire netting along the fence but even then, we didn't let her out into the garden on her own if we could help it. It was OK if Dan was there. We knew she would always be safe with him. He taught her what she could and could not do and, because she loved him with such a fierce passion, she never disobeyed him. Often, I would turn to Dan for his help if she was being particularly awkward. 'Dan, tell her, will you?'

He would call: 'Toadstool! Toadstool! Do as Ma says. Titch, don't be naughty.'

As Fleur grew older she would go in the boat with Dan. He taught her to row, although she was always too impetuous and heavy-handed and 'caught crabs' endlessly, the oar leaping into the air and out of her control. But he was patient, only laughing where others might have been irritated. He pretended to be cross if she refused to put a caught fish back, and on one occasion actually smacked her behind because she took a fish out of the bucket and ran into the house to show me, saying she had caught it. The fish died, of course, and then she was heartbroken. Sobbing and screaming uncontrollably.

Dan had a small biscuit tin with holes in for his worms and naturally Fleur had to have the same. Often you could see her in the garden hunting out worms for Dan, quite oblivious to any damage she might be doing to the lawn, but she always insisted on keeping them in her own tin. If she found an extra-juicy one, she didn't wait to put it in the tin but ran to find him with it dangling between her fingers, shrieking out with excitement. 'Well done, Titch. That is a good one. Now go and find some more.' He had his own ways of getting some peace.

Dan's other preoccupations were football and reading. He would kick a ball about in the garden, but more often he would go with his friends to the park. At these times, I would have my work cut out keeping Fleur busy until he returned. Reading was not such a problem, though because Dan wisely made a rule very early on that he would only read to her as long as she did not interrupt with questions, she would listen to anything. Once I came upon her listening to *The Life Cycle of the Mexican Lizard*! Dan simply read out loud whatever he was currently reading, sometimes Dickens, sometimes *Football News*. Fleur didn't care, providing she could sit cross-legged on his bed and be part of whatever he was doing. As a consequence, she learned to read herself very quickly and was reading her own books before she started school.

She was happy to go to school because she was familiar with

the building and with the teachers, as she went every day with me to meet Dan and as soon as the bell rang she would run to the school door to find him. Sometimes, impatient as usual, she would disappear inside. I used to laugh. How she found him I was never sure, but they would emerge hand in hand, she skipping and talking, with Dan trying hard not to look pleased. By the time she went though, Dan had moved to the grammar school, which was a short bus ride away. Fleur and I would walk with Dan as far as the bus stop in the mornings and then go on to her school. In the afternoons, I fetched her in the car and then drove to Dan's school. I needn't have done this, because Dan was just as capable of coming home from school as he was of going, but Fleur made such a fuss if we weren't going to pick him up that I generally gave in. If we were early I took her to a nearby park and duck pond and we would feed the ducks with crusts of bread. Meanwhile, in anticipation of seeing Dan, she talked faster and faster – never stopped.

I never quite knew what frame of mind Fleur would be when she came out of school. Always active, always talkative. Sometimes life was wonderful, sometimes 'vulgar'. Vulgar was a word she used frequently; she meant horrible or revolting. 'How was dinner today?'

'Vulgar!'

When the memory was returning, the reliving, I put my hand to my mouth, as if in shock. People must have noticed sometimes as I stood in a queue or suddenly stopped in the street or a shop or café and put my hand to my mouth. Anywhere, anytime, always unexpected, the memories rose up and my hand would go to my mouth.

Chapter 22

It was the day I stayed in bed with 'flu. I got up to get breakfast but couldn't keep still for the aching. I had to go back to bed. Peter said he would take the children to school. If he was late for work, too bad! He would arrange for Miss Watts to keep Fleur after school had finished, and Dan could fetch her and bring her home. He would phone me to confirm these arrangements. I kissed them goodbye and went back to bed. A few moments later, Peter returned and shouted that Dan had forgotten his football, then the door shut and the house was silent.

I only got up once to get a drink of orange, the day vanishing in a feverish, aching dream, but in the middle of the afternoon I woke. It was quarter to three. Fleur would be coming out in three-quarters of an hour, but I knew they would not be back till nearly five, so I went back to sleep.

When the front doorbell rang, I was glad. I didn't notice the time and even though I felt so unwell, I was excited, as I always was, to see the children after school. I opened the door with my arms ready as usual, ready for their hugs and chatter and saw, instead of the children, a strange woman standing on the doorstep, her face ashen, her voice shaking.

'There's been an accident. Please come quickly.' I had no need to ask – didn't want to ask – but grabbed a coat, which I slung over my nightdress, and ran with the woman to the waiting car. I lost track of the journey, seeing and yet not seeing. No one said a word. And I fought the hysteria.

Not far from Fleur's school was a crowd. People everywhere. A police car in the middle of the road. An ambulance. I jumped from the car before it had stopped, stumbled, someone pulled me up. I pushed my way forward through the crowd. Couldn't hear anything; it's never real, the silence and the slow motion.

All I saw was the red car. Dan lay in front of it, half in the road, half on the pavement. His body was contorted; blood was trickling from his nose. 'Don't touch him, please,' someone shouted. I took his hand and called to him.

'Don't touch him, please. Come on, now.'

I hadn't thought about Fleur at all until I saw the small body, entirely covered in a red blanket, being carried on a stretcher.

I know I was screaming and fighting to get to the stretcher, but my legs gave way. Someone caught hold of me, but I was so violent, so violently pushing everyone, everything away. They were in my way. Then with a fearful howl I hurled myself at the men with the stretcher. I couldn't see Fleur; I could only see the red blanket. I tore it away. And Fleur looked at me; her eyes wide open; a piece of chestnut hair had caught in her mouth. 'Flower!'

Someone said, 'There's nothing we can do here. See to the boy.'

Fleur, as planned, had waited with Miss Watts, helping her to tidy up, putting paints away, picking up bits and pieces. Miss Watts gave her a sheet of red sticky paper to take home. She had folded it carefully and put it in her purse, which hung round her neck. She was so excited that Dan was fetching her. She wanted to show him her sums.

Dan arrived at twenty past four. He came to her classroom and looked at all her books and her painting on the wall. She already had her coat on. They walked out through the school gates, Dan holding

Fleur with one hand and his football under his other arm. There were a lot of children about. Streams of boys from Dan's school, having arrived back by bus, were crowding along the pavements. There was a lot of shouting and laughter. Fleur was skipping and talking. Several of Dan's friends passed and several joked about him having to fetch his sister. Then one boy, fooling around, knocked the football out of Dan's arms; it rolled into the road. Fleur broke loose from Dan and ran after the ball for him. She didn't see the red car, but Dan did. He screamed and dived to get her, but it was too late. She was caught under the wheels of the car and killed outright. Dan was tossed up into the air and landed on his head. He was on a life-support machine for seven months before he died.

Fleur's funeral came and went but I, being totally absorbed with Dan, was hardly aware of it. I did go to the funeral, of course, but my whole being was at Dan's bedside. My body somehow went through the motions and Fleur, well, I couldn't register that she was dead. All my concentration and willpower now centred on Dan. All my prayers and faith in God. I was even cheerful, quite certain that my prayers would be answered. There was no way in my mind that this life, with all its potential, with all its love, could go from us. I talked to Dan continuously, read from his favourite books and the sport pages from newspapers. I brought in his Walkman so that he could listen to his tapes. He lay there with the earphones on, the Walkman on his pillow, perfectly still, and all the time the ventilator breathed for him. In-out, in-out. Please God, I want to take him home. Please.

I was convinced that at home he would regain consciousness. I obsessed about putting him in his boat and rowing him up the river. I knew the river, the sound of the oars in water, would wake him up. 'Is there any way I can take him home – put him in the boat?' I begged them. But the question was always answered with pitying eyes and shakes of the head. Mad woman, they thought, but understandably so.

Peter got agitated with me, by my continual insistence that everything would be all right, which created in him a complex response of anger and anxiety, yet I saw nothing of this at the time. Only later. Too much later. And so I did nothing, didn't follow my instincts, and instead left Dan in his hospital bed. Oh, what a terrible coward I was. I was the mother and I knew things they could have never known and I knew that Dan would come back to me if we went home. And yet I capitulated, did nothing. Hadn't made a scene, hadn't made a fuss. Oh God, I was so cowardly.

Now I suffered the torture of regret. Why had I been so cowardly? It would have saved him, but I hadn't the courage of my convictions. I had been too afraid, too afraid of being wrong, of being mad, of finding out that faith didn't work after all. Better not to know our ultimate nothingness. And so I remained by his bedside, changing his nappies, changing the saline bottles, becoming his full-time nurse. But I knew I was being tested and would be found wanting. If I failed him now, I could never, never in all eternity forgive myself, for, in the last analysis, I had been afraid of looking foolish, of being wrong. Frightened that my faith would not move mountains after all. Frightened of putting God to the test.

Peter, on the other hand, took a view that he described as realistic. He was resigned to losing his son and could not bear to see him for more than a few minutes at a time. Had it not been for me, he would hardly have gone to the hospital at all. My attitude drove him to desperation and, in his grief and driven by his sense of helplessness, he called me stupid and neurotic.

I had almost successfully wiped Fleur out of my mind. But as the months passed and Dan's condition deteriorated, I began longing for her. I was deserate for her help, as I was so sure that Dan would have woken up for her, with her loving, pixie-bright face, her unquestioning love. She would have demanded he come back to her. Demanded. Hands on hips! Yet how could she bear seeing him like that? Perhaps it was best she wasn't there.

One evening, I sat on the edge of his bed, stroking his hair. I held his hand. No response. He wasn't there. The ventilator breathed in-out, in-out, but he wasn't there. A wave of uncontrolable panic surged up into my throat and I felt myself slipping, slipping slowly, into a black uncontrollable panic. I shut my eyes and repeated, thoughtlessly, 'Our Father, which art in Heaven,' over and over again. But nothing. Nothing at all. I was alone and powerless. Powerless. God was not there to answer any prayers.

As they went to turn off the life-support system, I ran from the room. Ran from the hospital, didn't stay to say goodbye, to look. Nothing. I drove home, got right under the covers of our bed into complete darkness.

I woke to a dead soul housed inside a live body.

Chapter 23

After Dan's death, Peter tried to persuade me to go away with him, but I couldn't. He was kind, wanting to be close to me, but I avoided him. I couldn't have sex any more; I didn't dare allow myself to feel, either physically or mentally.

So I went back to part-time work at the hospital and was soon offered a full-time job as personal assistant to three consultants in the ophthalmology department. I joined the tennis club, although I hadn't played tennis for years; I went to art classes. Friends were kind and asked us out a lot. I entertained them in return, denying the emptiness of the house when they left. It was all a dream.

Peter couldn't bear my coldness, you see; it's perfectly understandable. He had to escape, I understand that now. I don't blame him at all for staying away and then preferring to be with someone else. I never blamed him. I was numb to it. But the beautiful house, Dan and Fleur's house, became unbearable. The river. The boat. The bedrooms were always tidy. There was nothing to do. No one to shop or cook for, no washing, ironing. I was an empty shell within an empty shell and in the end the house was sold; the boat was sold. I moved to where I am now and Peter remarried just afterwards. I sent him a card saying I would never again be as happy as I had been with him and the kids. And I was sorry. At least I did that.

You know, for a while I thought I'd cracked it, that I was doing really well. I was so busy. I never stopped. But then inevitably the exhaustion set in, so much so that I can remember the night I came back from work and sat in the chair, quiet, empty, but I not having to do anything. I didn't have to talk or be jolly or anything. I just sat there and I remember thinking, This is your home. You are safe here. I was too tired to run away any more. Even if it meant being alone for ever. That's how it felt, a strange kind of relief. From trying. So, home became a cave in which I could hide. In the end, home became a kind of escape and I went out less and less as feelings of panic connected with the outside became increasingly hard to control. Friends assumed that I was 'all right now', as I seemed more content to be at home. At work, I was as bright and breezy as ever, I'm sure that's true. Everyone knew, of course, but nothing was ever said. And the rawness disappeared and I thought about Dan and Fleur as if they belonged to another life, dispassionately.

When people asked me if I had any children, I always hesitated. If I said no, I was killing them off once more, denying them. If I told the truth: 'I had two children but they were both killed in a car accident,' the general responses of, 'Oh! I'm so sorry,' or, 'How dreadful!' were as vacuous as would be my retort of, 'Yes, pretty dreadful, really,' and so I avoided the questions at all costs.

For a time, I got into the habit of lying. Making up a complete life history for them both, based, of course, on what I guessed might well have been the truth, had they lived. That was rather fun; it brought them alive, made them people again. It was the only opportunity I had of referring to them, because those who knew never mentioned them. It was as if they had never existed. But with others? Strangers? How far would I be able to take the lies? It was all right pretending about such things as O levels and A levels; I might even get away with the university bit. 'Oh! reading theology at Leeds,' but then what? What about girlfriends and boyfriends, husbands, wives, children? Could I be the fictitious grandmother

I would like to be? Already at dinner parties I sat and listened as the chatting guests flaunted their various children. Masses of photographs passed round, school plays and choirs, sports medals and exam successes, holidays, parties and general get-togethers accompanied by detailed explanations of their 'funny little ways'. I had nothing to say. Nothing at all. And nobody seemed to notice.

Chapter 24

I looked at my watch; it was nearly ten o' clock. I lit another cigarette and blew a cloud of pale grey smoke into the air, where it moved slowly in the sunlight and then disappeared. From somewhere I could hear the sound of men's voices. If there was someone in the garden, I would ask if I could have a fork or a spade so I could weed some rose beds. I didn't want to sit doing nothing all day. Perhaps, too, they would like me better, notice me more if I did something for them.

I stubbed out the cigarette under my foot and threw the remains into the earth. The voices were getting fainter and so I hurried through the archway and saw two of the brothers standing by the cedar tree. They had their backs to me and appeared to be watching the rabbit, which was still tied to the tree. I recognised the young spotty brother at once, but the other one I wasn't so sure about. Was he one of those who had been reading in the library? In any case, neither of them turned towards me and so I had to speak to their backs.

'Hello! Good morning!' And then they turned without expression, as if they had known I was approaching them all the time. They didn't seem pleased.

'I was wondering – do you think I could have a spade or a fork or something? I thought I'd have a go at weeding in the rose garden.'

They stared at me, incredulous, and I wanted to laugh.

'That would be all right, wouldn't it? I like gardening and it'd give me something to do. That rose garden is a bit of a wreck, isn't it!' I shouldn't have said that.

'Well, I don't know.' It was the spotty one, and he clearly didn't know what to say. He turned. 'There are some things in the shed, aren't there? We're going there, anyway.'

The other nodded.

They led the way down by the visitors' block, passed my room and beyond, to a wild, nettle-ridden patch on the far side, where stood an old wooden garage.

The 'reading brother', as I thought of him, pulled open one of the double doors and the inside flooded with light. Against one wall leaned two bicycles with baskets hanging from the handlebars. Spiders' webs hung from the spokes of the wheels. The walls were lined with wide shelves on which lay wooden storage trays, but all they contained now were dry, wrinkled leaves and dust. Red clay flowerpots were piled in corners amongst seed trays and bean sticks. Along one side was a row of hooks from which hung various dog collars and leads. At the back there was a workbench and leaning against this were various gardening tools, but to reach them it was necessary to squeeze past the shiny green motor mower, which stood in the middle, looking quite out of place amongst the dust and the cobwebs.

'Give me a hand with this. Better open the other door.' And the spotty brother unbolted the second door and tugged it open. At once, hordes of brown lice scattered, disturbed by the moving doors. The two of them pushed out the mower and then almost simultaneously wiped the dust from their spotless habits. In contrast to the younger, rather gangling man with the acne-covered face, the other was handsome with his immaculately cut, thick wavy hair, his tall, stylish bearing and his habit,which hung elegantly down to the top of expensive leather shoes.

'Now, what exactly do you want?' The 'reading brother' sounded vaguely impatient. 'Have a look. There are various things here.' He led me to the back of the shed and picked up a fork. 'Will this do?'

'That's fine.' I took the fork from him. 'I'm afraid I don't know your names. I'm Rose Gregory.'

I looked at the faces, but the slight warmth I thought I had detected before, the warmth that encouraged me to ask their names, had gone. The man still standing beside me looked questionably towards his companion who said, 'Stephen,' and moved self-consciously towards a half-open toolbox standing in the nearby corner.

'I'm David,' said the other, and for a moment he actually looked at me! I know I smiled.

'Are you going to do some gardening, too?'

He shook his head. 'Mending the chicken run. Some of the wire needs replacing.'

'What? You keep chickens?' The idea pleased me. There was nothing more wonderful than collecting eggs. I had done it as a child when we had stayed on a farm for a few days. It was one of my happy childhood memories.

'Not now. Too many foxes about. Haven't had chickens since I've been here. Became a dogs' run.'

'What's it going to be for now – as you're mending it?'

'I don't think we're sure,' the good-looking one, David, mumbled, and actually gave a hint of amusement.

'It's not for Brother Joseph's rabbit, is it? Or is it?'

He shrugged. 'Not sure, as I said.'

I changed the subject. 'How long have you been here, then?'

'Six years,' and he turned away and joined Stephen by the toolbox.

'And you?'

'Just coming up to nine months.'

'Not long, then.' I wanted to ask if he was happy, if it was all right here.

'But we're moving in five weeks.' He sounded a bit despondent.

'I know. Do you mind?'

'It's worse for some of the others. The older ones. They feel they'll be leaving all their friends behind,' – and he pointed to beyond the Monks' Walk – 'in the graveyard. They don't want to leave because of that, do they?' He turned towards Brother David, who was sorting through a jar of nails.

'We've got a private graveyard, the other side of the walk. Perhaps you haven't seen it yet. Some of the old brothers like to go there to "talk to their friends". The move will be hard for them. It's not so bad for us.'

I wasn't sure whether he was mocking the old monks. Did they really think they were talking to their friends? Did they believe their friends could hear? Did they really believe? I never felt near to Dan or Fleur when I went to their little graves and so I've stopped going.

Brother David pointed to a roll of chicken wire, which was hanging from a hook in the wall.

'Bring that wire!'

He turned to me. 'Have you got everything, then? Only we must get on and mend this run before lunch.'

I picked up a wicker basket. 'I'll take this to put the weeds in, if that's OK.' I took the fork. 'I'll just put them back here when I've finished, shall I?' But they were already making their way back down the path.

'Thanks very much,' I called after them and then hoped they hadn't detected a smudge of sarcasm as I followed them into the sunlight. But as soon as I was some distance away, I heard them talking; one of them laughed.

Chapter 25

By the time I returned to the rose garden, my enthusiasm for weeding had gone. That tiredness came over me, so I stood staring at the weeds in the central bed, fork still in one hand and wicker basket in the other. If I stood still long enough, I would go to sleep.

But I made myself begin. I dropped the basket and began tickling the stony surface of the baked, crusted soil and then, without knowing, as if suddenly wound up, I plunged the fork into the earth rhythmically, mindlessly. The work was automatic, hypnotic, like the days of my life. I was programmed to perform quite well. Everything worked. I moved, spoke and smiled. The fork rang out as I plunged it against the tiny white stones that littered the dry earth. I thrust harder and harder, lifting, bending. Particles of earth spilt onto the crazy paving and my hair fell loose and into my eyes. The prongs of the fork dazzled in the sun and as I twisted my body to avoid the sharp thorns from a green sucker, I plunged the fork into my foot.

My yell of 'Shit!' bounced off the walls.

I hardly dare look at the fork prong, rigid and embedded just beneath my big toe, but I had to pull it out. I shut my eyes and pulled. I thought it would all go away if I started digging again, go on as if nothing had happened, but of course that doesn't work, does it? The nerves in my foot began to recover from the shock and the pain started.

I lifted my foot to somehow shake off the agony and blood was spurting onto the earth. The pain spread everywhere, so I hopped to the garden seat and rocked myself back and forwards in a kind of rhythm to ease the pain. I know I spoke to myself out loud, 'You bloody idiot.' And I knew I was going to have to do something. It was pouring blood, a bit scary. I had nothing with me to put round my foot so I half hopped, half limped back to the bathroom.

It was agony running the cold water over the deep hole, but nothing I could do would stem the bleeding and I had only bought a couple of handkerchiefs with me and these were quickly soaked in blood. Back in my room, I found my nylon tights and used them as a tight bandage, but the blood seeped through, so, short of tearing up a sheet or using another piece of clothing, there seemed nothing I could do.

Of course, I knew, with what I can only describe as shame, that I would have to go for help. Hadn't Father Godfrey said something about a doctor staying with them? Oh, God, really, that was the last thing I wanted to do. But the bleeding wouldn't stop and I began to feel sick and dizzy.

I leaned outside my door, eyes closed for a moment and when I opened them I saw Brother Joseph standing at the far end of the path, staring at me. It was a relief to see it was him. Somehow it didn't seem so bad asking him for help, so I called, my voice horribly shrill in that quiet place. The brother jerked into action, like a puppet on a wire, and ran towards me, dragging the rabbit behind him.

He didn't notice my bleeding foot; he was too interested in looking into my face and grinning up at me. His eyes blinked rapidly. 'I was coming to find you,' he panted. 'Were you looking for me?' His watery blue eyes longed for me to say, 'Yes.'

'You've come at exactly the right moment.' I knew that would please him. 'Can you help me, please? Look, I've hurt my foot. I need a plaster or something.'

He looked to where I was pointing and stared, then turned

without a word, and quickly jogged away towards the house, stopping once to see if I was following. He could have been leading me to some priceless treasure, he looked so pleased with himself.

He disappeared into the house and by the time I reached the French windows he was nowhere to be seen. My foot was trailing blood and throbbing badly and I was irritated. Where was he, for goodness sake? The blood was seeping through the tights and I didn't like to go into the house and drip it all over the place. I wanted to cry. But at that moment Brother Joseph reappeared with someone.

'She's hurt her foot. She's hurt her foot. Dear, dear dear dear.' And he patted my arm as he stared earnestly at the blood. I could feel the heat of his body.

'What have you been doing with yourself, then? That's a nasty gash.' And the man in the jacket I had seen at breakfast knelt to unwind the tights. He looked up at me and smiled. 'Wait a minute while I fetch some dressing.' He walked back the way he had come, almost casually.

The rabbit was sniffing at the blood and I tried to hold it off by pulling hold of the lead.

'Come away, Francis. Leave it alone.' Joseph chuckled. 'Poor Francis got to sleep outside now, haven't you?'

He looked so hopefully at me, but I couldn't concentrate on anything for the pain in my foot.

'Got to go into the old dogs' run, haven't you?' he repeated.

'Oh dear,' was all I could manage.

'We're not very happy about that, are we Francis?' And then, 'You like it in my room, don't you?'

Thankfully, the man returned with a bundle of cotton wool. With this he mopped up the dripping blood and then, fixing a lump of it over the wound, he took me by the arm and guided me through the door, past the dining room and kitchen to a little room that had in earlier days been a pantry.

Inside was just like the school sickroom. There was a camp bed with a pillow and grey blanket folded at one end, a small, light brown wooden table and two chairs, and the walls were lined with white cupboards. There were some scales on the floor by the window and in one corner a washbasin.

'Do you want to lie down?'

'This is fine.' And I sat on the chair. I knew, of course, that he was the doctor. 'Sorry to be such a pest.'

'How on earth did you do it?'

I tried making a joke out of it and he laughed, an ugly guffaw that quite unsuited his dark, musical voice.

He knelt beside me, eased my sandal off, now discoloured and sticky. They were ruined, and I liked those sandals too! He lifted my foot and began to clean the gash. 'Well, this is not a very good start to your stay, I must say.' And there was that sensuous tone again, always on the edge of laughter.

He poured some water into a stainless-steel bowl, adding some disinfectant, which he took from one of the cupboards.

I watched him watch me. I think I must have gone white, because I was feeling faint.

'I think you should lie down,' he said and helped me from the chair to the patients' couch.

'Sorry to be such a nuisance,' I said again, and then wished I hadn't.

'You'll have to have a tetanus injection,' he said as he finished dressing my foot. 'When did you last have one?'

'When I was about six months old, I should think.'

He laughed. 'Thought as much. It's not something we bother about until something like this happens. Well, that's all right, because I can do it for you.'

He went to one of the cupboards and took out a small vial and placed it on the table. From another cupboard he took out a white plastic dish, a syringe in paper and a needle capped in a blue sheath.

He put everything into the plastic dish, then took out some squares of disinfectant tissue. He washed his hands, dried them carefully and then proceeded to fix the needle into the syringe. He had fine hands, strong and skilful, and he radiated confidence. There was something presumptuous about him, which both attracted and repelled me. I wanted to provoke him, to challenge him. I don't know why. I examined him closely as he pushed the needle into the rubber cap of the vial and drew up the liquid. He was extraordinary, both attractive and strange-looking at the same time. He was tall and wide-shouldered with straight brown hair cut in an uneven fringe over his high forehead, but growing thick and long into his nape. His face was round, almost podgy and his large brown eyes stared out from behind round wire glasses.

'Roll up your sleeve, please.'

He wiped the top of my arm with one of the antiseptic squares and then, holding the skin tightly between his fingers of one hand, he pushed the needle into my arm and slowly squeezed the plunger until all the liquid had gone. He placed another square over the spot where the needle was before pulling it out and pressing the square onto my arm.

'Hold that for a moment.'

'Ten out of ten!' I mocked.

'What?'

'It's a family joke.'

'Oh! I scored high, did I?'

I didn't want to smile.

'You've got mud on your face.' And he began to wipe my forehead and then my chin with the antiseptic squares. I noted his shoulders and the nape of his neck. He was so sure of himself. I liked that.

'How's the foot now?' he asked, and I sat up as he pulled his chair up to the couch.

'Well, it's throbbing, I must say. My whole foot's dropping off, I think!'

'Look, I'm going to give you a couple of painkillers and then I want you to lie down for a bit. Don't come for lunch. I'll have something sent over.'

There he was, bossing me about, and there seemed no point in arguing. I wanted to ask him what he was doing in this place. Normally I would have done, but I did feel extremely tired, my energy had gone for the moment.

Chapter 26

He walked with me to the lobby without taking my arm this time; he simply walked beside me with his hands in his pockets. He had a slow, leisurely gait and I guessed he was gearing his pace to match mine. My foot was throbbing badly, now that I was walking, but I didn't say anything. I felt less tense once we were out of that small room. Now we could speak without actually looking at each other.

Expecting him to leave me at the entrance to the gardens, I turned to thank him, but he touched my elbow through the open windows saying he would see me safely 'home'. Again, that faintly amused tone – yet with an authority that I obviously needed, although I couldn't have expressed it or consciously realised it then. But it was there and it had some kind of effect on me. Like a father, perhaps.

The heat outside really hit me after the coolness of the house and in the bright light the cedar tree stood exceptionally dark and solid above the sunlit lawn. The rabbit was nowhere to be seen, although there were still scraps of carrot and potato peelings dotted near the tree.

'Why has the rabbit got to sleep in the chicken run now?' The question was out before I knew I was speaking, but it diluted the tension of our togetherness.

'Ah! Brother Joseph.' He hesitated. 'That's a difficult one.' He was being diplomatic and cagey and it annoyed me.

'He's obviously upset about it.' I think I snapped a bit, as if it was his fault. 'He might pretend otherwise, but you can see that he's not all that thrilled about it.'

I did look at him then, and realised that I didn't know his name. In any case, he was ignoring the rabbit business, obviously didn't want to be drawn over it. And I felt even more annoyed. 'Why isn't it OK in his room? Apparently, it always has been. I know—'

'It's the smell.' And then, 'I don't really think a bedroom is the best place for a rabbit to be, do you?'

The tone was patronising. He was clever, throwing the question back at me.

'I feel sorry for him, that's all. What can he do against all you big, strong, clever people? Not a lot. What's your name, by the way?'

He laughed and told me Guy Harwood, but they called him Dr Guy.

'You are a doctor, then? Just wondered.'

He laughed again. I don't know why he kept laughing.

'Yes, I'm a doctor.'

'Why are you here?'

He said something like, 'Long story. Not for now, for another time, perhaps,' and I wished I hadn't asked, because his manner changed, became not so relaxed and his voice wary. He didn't like the question and I felt awkward. I told myself that I couldn't care less if he didn't want to say. Yet, really, I was struck by his flirtatious protectiveness, as if, somehow, we had a shared past. I knew he was staring down at me and so I glared ahead as if deep in thought, hiding my feelings, denying him my eyes, which might give things away.

'And what about you?' he asked suddenly.

'That's a long story too.'

'So, it looks as if we're going to have to have a long session some time!'

His presumption and laughing voice were hard to bear.

We had nearly reached my room, which was now in shadow, and it was cooler walking along the shady path.

'How's the foot?'

'Swelling nicely, thank you.'

We stopped for him to examine the puffy flesh, which bulged up either side of the bandage. It was a sight, and his laughter was both reassuring and sympathetic.

'The bandage will help that a bit, but I think I'll take a look at it after lunch. I would lie down for a little.'

He was serious for the first time and I knew that I must have looked pale. I was very tired.

He opened the door of my room and stood in the doorway watching as I sat on the bed.

'Have a rest,'he said, 'And I'll have something sent over for your lunch.'

'Look, please don't trouble. I'm not hungry. And don't worry any more. I'll be fine. Try to keep out of the way,' I joked.

'We'll see.' He studied me closely and then smiled. He pulled off the top covers. 'Come on, lie down.'

It was like being a child again.

Chapter 27

The Angelus rang for Matins, but for once Guy didn't want to go; Rose Gregory would be the excuse. Instead, he decided to walk the avenue, something he hadn't done for ages.

When he had first come, he thought that he would often be walking this lane between the beech trees, but there never seemed time, what with his role as house doctor and handyman, for he was clever with plumbing and electrical gadgets, and there was always something that needed repairing. And then the fetching and carrying; he was the only one who could drive a car. But the fact was that he always happier when he was busy. Despite all this, he'd had the time he needed to do some serious thinking and had decided that, after all, he must return to general practice. It was ironic – one of the reasons he had wanted to leave his work as a GP, take this sabbatical, was because he too often felt inadequate. Helpless at times. There had been so much pain and suffering he had been incapable of alleviating. He had found the whole business deeply disturbing, thought he was inadequate as a doctor. And he didn't do failure very well.

'I'm risk-averse,' he said out loud. 'Anything to avoid failure. Coward!'

He had always excelled in everything he did and his seniors and peers alike recognised him as especially gifted. This made him who he was. Perhaps because of this, he couldn't bear to fail. He remembered his moods and sulks if he failed at anything. He had walked out of that card game once because he was losing! And yet it was nothing to do with having to win, but to do with vulnerability, to do with lack of control, to do with self-esteem. More like pride before a fall, he thought. He had spent many hours questioning why he should be as he was. Now he had more or less accepted himself for who he was, how he was, and realising that he was unlikely to change now, had learned to avoid situations he couldn't control as far as possible.

But before, as a GP, his frustrations grew and he had convinced himself that medicine was the wrong profession for him. Tom in particular argued that it was the exhaustion that was undermining his confidence, but nevertheless he left the practice and went to Australia to stay with friends, which irritated his father, who thought him weak and foolish. My father! What can I say? he thought with a wry smile to himself.

As a boy, his precociousness had been a source of parental pride, a cleverness for which his father took credit. But as he grew tall and strong, and his voice broke and he was no longer a child but an intelligent young man, his father became increasingly judgemental and his mother's love for him became, for his father, a constant irritation. He was jealous of me, Guy thought, shrugging, for he understood this now but at the time it had been a mystery and a source of constant friction. Then Guy responded the only way he could: by challenging his father's intellect, his logic, his wisdom, and he became obsessed with winning every argument, every game, every problem, and learned to avoid all those areas he couldn't be master over. Risk-averse. 'Avoid at all costs.' He spoke out loud again as he thought of Rose Gregory. And this accepting attitude was symbolised by the casual shrug of the shoulders that had become his trademark, along with his unhurried movements and apparently pragmatic approach to life.

However, he was grateful to his father – who had known Godfrey from their student days – for suggesting this place. Godfrey often shared his problems with the old and the sick – and the not so old – with Guy's father. He received one letter in which Godfrey described the monks' difficulties in coping with one of the older members of the community, who had had a breakdown and was very unwell. He had written some details about the dog kennels and how they were allowing the ailing monk to breed cocker spaniels. His father wrote to Guy in Australia and suggested he offered Godfrey some help for a time.

It was fortunate that Godfrey welcomed him as he did. To all intents and purposes he was a novice, and there was no doubt that Godfrey had hoped very much that he would go on to take his vows and was disappointed when he told him he'd decided to return to general practice when he left them. Of course, he couldn't make everything right for his patients; all he could do was his best and that had to be good enough. One had to take some risks in life; he didn't need to constantly beat himself up about failure.

The irony was that this fear of failure would, of course, cause him to lose much, most particularly in the area of relationships, especially with women. Can't go through that again, he was thinking. The one time he had risked it, the only time, it didn't work out, so never again. That was real failure. Deep, cutting, 'I don't want you' failure. So never again. He thought about Rose and decided he must take her painkillers. He would fetch some from the surgery as soon as he got back. She was in a lot of pain; he could see it in her face.

He walked on to the old dog kennels. The area was unkempt. Brambles straggled through the long grass, and the rhododendron and hazel saplings, which surrounded the place, had grown to form thick cover. It was now impossible to find the paths that had once led to the wooded area beyond. He examined the run and noticed the new wire battened to pale, fresh timber. They had made a good job of it. The hinges on the gate had been renewed too. It now stood shut but not locked. There was a homemade wire hook that fixed into a coupling, but now it hung stiff and still on the gatepost. He tested the gate for solidity and yes, although it could only be opened with difficulty because of the thick clumps of grass, it was strong and sound. He pushed the gate shut and placed the wire hook into position; it slotted in well. The place was safe enough, he thought. And the wire high enough to deter foxes. Foxes could be a menace, apparently.

He recalled Rose's concern. It was true the brothers treated the rabbit as a joke; Joseph was a joke. He had seen and heard them. Rose, even in the short time she had been here, showed sympathy, seemed concerned. Strange, that.

He, personally, had not minded one way or the other – the rabbit in Joseph's room or in the run – it was all the same to him, but Bertram seemed to have a thing about it. However, he thought Bertram was overreacting when he argued so vociferously that the attention given to the animal undermined Brother Joseph's devotional life – what a load of rubbish – and that the absurdity of a monk trailing a rabbit around on a lead reflected on them all and on the monastic life as a whole. Pompous ass! Guy had never taken part in these discussions, not considered it to be his business, but now he thought about Rose. She had picked up a situation in a matter of hours, something the rest of them had not realised over months.

He shook his head and smiled to himself. She would be quite a match for Bertram. And in any case, he didn't think Bertram's preoccupation was really about the rabbit at all. But he wasn't going to get involved one way or the other, for surely this issue was of no real consequence. How could it matter, in the great scheme of things, whether Guy avoided the rabbit question or not? There were, after all, far more important things to concern him. He would rather think about the woman. There was something about her.

What was she doing here, really?

As he crossed the lawn back to the house, he turned to look in the direction of her room. He couldn't see it from where he was but he looked anyway, wondering if she was still resting, and remembered that he must organise some lunch for her. He would take it himself with the painkillers and then he could check on her foot again. Why did he rather look forward to that?

Chapter 28

After Matins, the monks made their way to Father Godfrey's study for the customary pre-lunch sherry, a weekly event he had instigated but that for several years now he rather regretted. None of them was easy with informal chatter and Godfrey found himself left with the onerous responsibility of making it jolly. The whole thing was exceedingly tiresome. However he had been assured by Brother Bertram, when he had suggested abandoning the event, that the brothers would be very disappointed and looked forward to their chats very much. Godfrey thought it was more likely to be the sherry that they would miss and this he could well understand, as he suspected that he was not the only member of the community to keep a bottle on hand.

He had left his door ajar, as usual, and began pouring out the sherry into the small glasses he kept in the corner cupboard. Well, at least this morning he would have something definite to talk about, as there was so much to organise. He wondered how the attic sorting-out was coming along. He would have to go up there himself this afternoon. Which reminded him: he must ask Brother Bertram if he and Brother Oswald had sorted out the valuable books from the library. Bertram had been so preoccupied with the business of the rabbit, he might well have forgotten.

Brother Bertram really was a thorn in his side. The trouble

was, it was hard to fault him; he was always so reasonable and he was, strictly speaking, quite right about the rabbit but Godfrey doubted whether any of the others would have bothered had not he stirred things up. He seemed to have it in for Brother Joseph. The phrase 'sure, he is an honourable man' came into his mind. In addition, Bertram had Oswald as his staunch ally and everyone liked Oswald for his quiet, kindly ways. Chameleon-like, he blended into any situation and, because he was so agreeable and so devoted to Bertram, everyone accepted that Bertram must be agreeable too. Sometimes Godfrey wondered about the nature of that friendship, but oh well, what the eye didn't see, the heart couldn't grieve over, and he didn't believe in looking for trouble.

He didn't want any trouble with Brother Joseph either. Pray Heaven he accepted the new arrangements. Anyway, Mrs Gregory would keep Joseph occupied for a day or two, hopefully. Godfrey sighed. He had had no time to see Mrs Gregory today, and this afternoon would be busy with the attic business, and yet he had promised to show her the rest of the garden. Perhaps Joseph could do that and he would try to think of something for tomorrow. But he knew it was uncharitable of him to foist Joseph on her.

Hearing the brothers' footsteps coming up the corridor, Godrey gulped some sherry from the glass in his hand, quickly refilled it, and then placed himself by the window and arranged a 'welcoming look' on his face.

'Come in, come in. Help yourselves to a sherry.' He indicated the tray of glasses before flicking the lock of hair out of his eyes.

Bertram always came in first. Today he was followed by Brother Joseph, for whom this was a new experience. This, at any rate, was some consolation for not working in the kitchen. The kitchen staff were always too busy getting Sunday roast to enjoy the sherry party. Today Joseph would have been first had not Bertram manoeuvred himself into that position with a firm, 'Excuse me, Brother!' and, picking up a glass, advanced on Godfrey, leaving Joseph grinning at the sherry glasses uncertainly. Having examined the sherry carefully, he picked up one in his quivering hand and passed it to Oswald, who had followed them in.

'Have one yourself, Brother,' Oswald said, but Joseph shook his head and giggled, taking upon himself the task of handing a sherry to each brother as he came into the room, and so replicating the joy of serving, which the kitchen work had given him for so many years.

'We've mended the run for you, Brother.' Stephen's rather high voice made Joseph jump. 'You'll be able to put your rabbit there tonight.'

Joseph put down the glass he was holding and looked up at the spotty, ginger-haired youth. His smiled disappeared momentarily, and then he turned away as if hadn't heard.

Father Godfrey interrupted the low, hesitant mutterings by raising his voice slightly, 'Just a word, please. Brother Bertram assures me that you all know what you are doing this afternoon. I shall come up to the attic myself at some stage. Could I ask you all to work as speedily as possible so that we are ready for the Philips man tomorrow. I need not remind you what little time we have left before the move. And, by the way, we shall need a large box or boxes to put the books in, so could someone please sort that after luncheon.'

He paused and looked down at his empty glass. 'And apparently,' – this was a little piece of information that Bertram had dropped on him – 'Dr Guy, unusually, did not attend Matins this morning. Does anyone know where he is? He's not unwell I hope, or locked in the attic!' The small joke was greeted by silent faces and Godfrey mourned their lack of humour. He waited as a matter of courtesy but he didn't expect any response. Only Bertram knew anything, but preferred to inform him at private meetings. Gives him a sense of power, Godfrey thought. He was surprised, therefore, when Joseph waved his hands and shuffled towards him.

'He's looking after the lady,' he announced with some excitement.

'She hurt herself.'

'She's what? What do you mean?'A wave of intense irritability engulfed him. 'What do you mean, Brother?'

Joseph began a long ramble which Godfrey, wearied beyond words, interrupted with, 'Yes, yes, thank you,' and then muttered, 'we could do without any more problems, I should think.' He sighed with exasperation. 'If you see Dr Guy before I do,' Godfrey said weakly, 'please ask him to come to me.'

After they had gone, Godfrey sat for a moment and gazed out of the window that overlooked the front of the house. He saw Rose's car and groaned, running his hand across his forehead. She was just an added problem! It was a pity he had ever said yes to her. They really didn't have time for anything extra – and now this. What on earth was she doing gardening, for goodness sake? Of course, the loss of her children was quite dreadful, but it was three years ago, she must be – well, not getting over it exactly, but adjusting, coming to terms, and so on.

So, what did she want from them now? People who came to stay were usually looking for something, hoping to find some instant nirvana. But they came in groups. He had never been that keen on having women, anyway; only financial needs demanded it, but one on her own was doubly awkward. Thankfully, though, she appeared self-assured and independent; too independent, it seemed. Yet, despite that, there was that look about her. Was it tiredness? Was it…?

The memory of his dream of Padma and India retuned and left him with a vague sense of anxiety. But he was too absorbed with his own mortality; making sense of his life and facing his own death was enough; there was no energy left to take on problems belonging to someone else, although he knew he should. Everyone had to cope for himself; it was between him and God.

And the brothers, too, were silent within themselves, preoccupied. With what? Trying to convince themselves that it was not all some enormous hoax? Deadening feelings against that awful possibility that life was futile, that everything came to nothing? But if visitors were to find anything here, it would have to be some kind of spiritual thing; there was nothing any of them could actually do. Oh Lord, he thought, it had all seemed so clear years ago, giving and loving and doing and being. With age, it became unclear and uncertain. So where was all the wisdom that was supposed to be the compensation for old age? The only compensation he could think of was a kind of acceptance, and that came from loss of energy. A pretty negative sort of compensation.

He heard the bell ring for lunch. Let's hope it's a good roast, he thought. At least there's still food to enjoy.

Doctor Guy was waiting outside the dining room.

'Is everything all right? You missed Matins.'

'Yes. Sorry. Bit of an accident, I'm afraid.'

'So, I hear. Apparently Mrs Gregory hurt her foot.'

''Fraid' so. Put the prong of a garden fork through it. It's quite nasty, actually. I've dressed it for her. She's gone to lie down.'

Godfrey heaved a sigh. 'What about her lunch, then?'

'I'll take her something later, if that's all right.'

'You can cope, then? Well done! Well done!' Godfrey's attempt to disguise his exasperation was unsuccessful.

He shook the hair out of his eyes and stared at Guy uncertainly. He turned to go into the dining room and then said, suddenly, 'Better ask Brother Joseph to do it. He's supposed to be looking after her at the moment.' And, as an afterthought, 'Come to my room after lunch, will you? I'd better fill you in about Mrs Gregory.'

The brothers watched the conversation going on outside from under their brows and then waited patiently while the father abbot took his place in the centre of the top table. Grace said, they all sat, and Brother David commenced the reading.

Father Godfrey looked at the space left for Rose Gregory and felt a tinge of regret. Now and again there did seem something reassuring about having a woman sit at table. It lent a sense of harmony, of balance, but he couldn't think why this should be so. He had never consciously felt this before. Surely, after all these years, he could not be missing his mother. That was ridiculous! And yet in his old age he had to admit he sometimes yearned to have the comfort of a woman. Perhaps all old people felt like that. At any rate, it was not he that needed the comfort now but rather Mrs Gregory, so, if Dr Guy was seeing to her foot, he might as well also take the opportunity to – well – deal with the other matter, her problems whatever they were. He was a Doctor, after all. And he had the time.

He sighed. Yes, he certainly had more time .

Chapter 29

Staring at Godfrey through his round glasses, Guy listened carefully as Father Godfrey recounted all he knew about Rose Gregory. And he was shocked. 'Right. Well, thank you for telling me,' he said before leaving the room.

Now, walking back to his room, he began to worry. He was going to have to be involved and he wasn't sure he wanted to be. But in a way it was too late, and there could be no excuses now. No lack of time. Not too busy. But what, if anything, should he, could he, do? This personal involvement frightened him and, wanting to escape it, to think about something else, he decided to clean his car. Anything.

The somewhat shabby Ford was his and he had been allowed to keep it at the abbey so that it could be used for fetching and carrying, mostly eggs and vegetables from the local farm. Now he carried from the kitchen a bucket of soapy water and a sponge, which he put down beside the bonnet. There was no one around and there was that strange quietness one associates with Sunday afternoons. He slowly stroked the bonnet with the soapy sponge and the grey suds dripped off the car onto the ground at his feet. He was anxious and he knew he had that sulky look.

He thought about Rose and knew now that he had been right in suspecting she was a troubled woman. It had been obvious to him from the first that she was very defended, tense and anxious. Her quips and almost flirtatious sarcasm had not fooled him. He thought she was lovely, though, with her pale freckles and chestnut eyes. Yet it seemed she was trying to be something or someone else; what he knew about her now gave him a clearer understanding. The temporary amnesia? Well, that was a common post-trauma syndrome but to be taken seriously, nonetheless. Why hadn't her doctor or friends seen it coming? But he smiled wryly to himself, knowing that she was the very worst kind of person to try to help. He suspected that she could be extremely difficult. And now he was involved and he was a doctor, so there could be no excuses.

He leaned his arm on the top of the car and the sponge dripped from his other hand. Despite his concern, he recognised a certain excitement about the challenge. He knew now too, that it was medicine that he was looking forward to getting back to. There was much more to medicine than just healing the body, and perhaps the other kind of healing was even more important. One must find time for that.

He wrung out the dirty water from the sponge and started to wipe round the wheels. He was wasting his time, he knew, because they would get filthy again at the farm. He stopped and gazed over the top of the car to the trees beyond. He could take Rose with him, couldn't he, take her out for a drive to the farm? And for a cream tea? That's what he would do. It would get them out of everyone's way as well, especially as the Auction man was coming. Was the name Philips? – anyway, they were all in a flap about that.

No, he wouldn't say anything this evening; he would just dress her foot and chat and let things take their natural course. Perhaps she would tell him her story of her own accord. And then what? What should he do? What could he say? He must avoid an emotional scene. But she wasn't like that; that's why he was so drawn to her. She was like him: private, self-sufficient. She would never expect or need others to share her private world. Quite right too, and that way it was so much easier to keep relationships under control. Still, as a doctor he would try to win her confidence.

Now that he had decided some course of action, he felt better. The cleaning of the car took on some significance, and he would even do the inside. It was dreadfully dirty, covered with patches of dried mud and bits of straw and on the back seat were piles of empty egg boxes and some greasy tools wrapped in newspaper. He wanted it to be decent for the woman. He raised his eyebrows wryly at his anticipation.

He took back the bucket and sponge to the kitchen and found a black plastic bag, which he intended to fill with all the rubbish from the car. As he stood by the window wondering if, with an extension lead, he could hoover out the inside, he saw Brother Joseph crossing the lawn with a large cardboard box in his arms – the rabbit's box, obviously – and heading for Rose's room. 'Leave her alone, man,' he thought. 'Leave her alone.'

Chapter 30

After Guy, had gone, I lay counting the throbs of my aching foot. I couldn't sleep and so I found a cigarette and, lying back, puffed great clouds of smoke into the room. I couldn't relax. I was a bit – not sure of the right word – unsettled, the sort of feeling you get when you are waiting for something. As if something was in the air, so to speak. And it had to do with Guy, but I wasn't sure what it was.

I did eventually fall into a deep sleep and when I woke I felt an unaccustomed lightness, a kind of strange hopefulness, although my foot was hurting badly. I looked at my watch and was amazed to see it was half-past two already.

He hadn't come with my lunch, as promised. I decided he had probably forgotten, or was too busy, and was disappointed if I'm honest, but I told myself: Who cares, anyway.

I remember shrugging my shoulders and getting off the bed as if to do something distracting. I thought, I will not sit here waiting; I must do something. Not be here. Be busy. Not waiting for anything or anyone. But what? Go to the garden and fetch the fork and basket – tidy up. Could I walk that far? Yes. In any case and in some bizarre way I welcomed the physical pain because it was real and a distraction. I could concentrate on the pain and not think about anything else.

Sitting on the edge of the bed, I thought how many times, for how many hours had I sat just like this, sat and stared, frozen in inactivity. I used to think that if I sat quite still, mindless, I could take myself out of life, waiting to be found. I looked at the crucifix on the wall, arms outstretched and, crazily, I wanted someone, arms outstretched, to ask me to dance!

I must have been feeling better, because I did get up and made for the garden, limping slowly; I mustn't do any further damage or make matters worse; didn't want Guy to think me stupid and attention-seeking.

The basket and spade were where I'd left them and I noticed the mess I'd made. There were particles of earth thrown all over the place. I bent and swept the granules back onto the bed with my hands, but black spots spun in front of my eyes and I had to give up and sit down in the shade of a holly tree that stood on the other side of the wall.

We had had a holly tree in our hedge at home, but it never had berries and I had to make red bows to put amongst the sprigs of holly at Christmas. Fleur always demanded to be in charge of the decorations, but by the time we had lifted her onto chairs or held her up to reach, it made a long job of it. If anyone so much as changed the position of a bauble on the tree she noticed and wasn't pleased. It was difficult, because all her baubles were hung so low to the ground the cat played with them and knocked them off.

At Christmas, I indulged all my sentimental, romantic childhood fantasies. I strove to create the Christmas-card Christmas, and like a child, I longed for snow.

One Christmas it did snow. It started snowing while we were in church and we emerged to swirling, fat snowflakes and to pealing bells. Perfect! Then I would have conjured, if I could, ladies in long dresses and muffs, gentlemen with top hats and silver-knobbed walking sticks, happy children with coloured scarves and boots. Even the dogs would have been nosing and barking through the snow. But what I could do to bring alive my fairy-tale Christmas,

I did. The house was filled with holly, ivy, silver balls, bells and red bows. There were walks with a basket to collect kindling for the open fires. The silver and copper shone in the firelight and candles were lit as we became more and more excited. Now I am amazed at my sentimentality. But then it had been for the children; precious memories from childhood, I thought, that they could carry with them always. And it was always so flat after Christmas, when the tree came down and the house was cleared of cards and decorations. Then the house stood bare and colourless. Had it been worth it?

Imagine that your child has fallen down a very deep, very narrow well-shaft. He is stuck far down and cannot move. You can just see the top of his head and you can hear him crying, 'Mother, Mother,' but you can't get down to him. You can only stand and listen. That is all you can do. I read something like that in the newspaper, once.

I'd been sitting with my eyes shut, but I opened them abruptly because I began to shiver as if I were cold, just for a second, and I wondered if anyone had come to see me, to bring me some lunch. He'd said he would.

I got back into my room, having dumped the fork and basket outside the door, and saw a tray with a plate of sandwiches, a banana and a glass of milk. So he had brought me some lunch then, after all. And I'd not been there. I hate milk like that, but I suppose he thought it would be good for me. They were ham sandwiches, quite OK, and actually I was hungry, I realised.

I had my mouth full when someone hammered on the door. No, it wasn't Guy, but Joseph and his rabbit. I wanted to tell him to go away, thinking, Why does it always have to be you? but he looked so pleased to see me, I had to smile.

'I brought your lunch.'

'Thank you very much.'

'I've got his box here,' he said.

The box was full of filthy straw and bits of newspaper. He noticed my face.

'I'm going to put clean stuff in.'

'Good.'

'Do you want to come?'

I really didn't want to. 'All right, if you want me to. Just let me finish this.'

He waited while I finished the sandwich and then, nodding, he picked up the box and hurried off towards the shed. I took the banana with me and cursed to myself as I followed him. I watched as he tipped out the dirty straw onto a compost heap, which was piled high behind the shed, and as wisps of straw caught the edge of his sleeve and the side of his habit.

'You've got some straw on you,' I said, but he only chuckled.

'It's good for the garden.' He stared at me again. He was always staring with his face close to mine.

'Muck! It's called muck.' And with that he turned back to the shed.

Leaning in the back corner was a half-used bale of straw and he tore handfuls from it and tossed them into the box. He's lonely, I thought, amongst all these brothers, he's lonely. He was frail and silly-looking, dirty and a bit smelly, but watching him, I was sad for him.

'Where's the box going?' I asked, although I knew.

'In the run.'

I followed him back down the path.

'They were Billie's.'

'Billie?'

'Had his dogs there.'

'What?'

We'd reached my room and I stopped by the door.

'He was ill. He had his dogs there. Puppies – little, like Francis.'

I think he wanted me to say something.

'We were always together, to be sure. I want to be with him again.' His face was creased with hopeful expectation. 'I wish I was dead like him.' He threw back his head and roared with laughter.

It was an ugly laugh and embarrassed me. I didn't feel able to say anything; I didn't feel very well, anyway.

'Where is Francis?' I asked, guilty at not wanting to talk about his friend Billie and the dogs and his dying and all that, and he pointed in the direction of the tree.

'Are you coming?' he asked again.

'I won't just now. My foot really is hurting a lot.'

'Later, then? To put him to bed?'

I just couldn't say no. 'We'll see,' but I knew I wouldn't. Still, he nodded with satisfaction and trotted off down the path.

I lay on the bed feeling empty and depressed. There was nothing to do and nothing I wanted to do. I thought about Guy and then was annoyed with myself. I didn't want to think about him. He had just been doing a job, nothing more. I wouldn't let anything else come into my head: certainly not some stranger who happened to bandage up my foot. Yet there was something about him, something that made me feel safe, like a child again. He appeared relaxed, unfazed, moving calmly, easily. That must have been part of it; there was something easy about him. I didn't have to pretend. I could be myself with him. Was it just that he was a doctor? And yet I had never been one of those who put doctors on a pedestal – apart from my father, of course. After all, I worked with them, I knew too much from the inside, so surely it couldn't be something as idiotic as 'doctor worship'?

Anyway, his looks were peculiar, with his round face and staring eyes. But his voice: soft and throaty with that touch of laughter. And when he had something to do, he did it with serious concentration, I'd noticed.

Dear God what was happening to me? Was I so needy? Perhaps, deep down, well hidden down. Yet how could I ever allow myself to feel anything for Guy? It was the most appalling betrayal. Dan. Fleur.

I remembered my only dream of Dan. He was sitting on the edge of my bed and I sat up and put on the light. He had put his arms round me. No honestly, I am not exaggerating. I felt them, actually felt him just as he always felt when he put his arms so firmly round me, as if he were the grown-up. I clung to him, felt his arms around me. 'Don't worry, Mum,' he said. 'I am not going to leave you at the moment. I'll stay with you.' And then he walked away down a long, dark corridor, and as he got to the end of it and was disappearing, he looked back and called: 'I have to go here. I don't want to, Mum, but don't worry, I won't leave you for a bit.'

I suppose I woke, but the bedside lamp was on and there was a dip in the bed where he must have been sitting for that moment. 'He's been here. He's been here, to me.' And then I cried, but with a kind of joy.

Fleur came to me in the boat. It was strange that it was she who came in the boat, but that was how it was. She was rowing very well all on her own and steered the boat into our landing stage, smiling that pixie grin, which she smiled whenever she was doing something she knew she shouldn't do but knowing that I would love her anyway. She knew that, no matter what, I would be overjoyed to see her. It was a heavenly smile. Then I noticed water in the bottom of the boat and around her feet. 'You'll catch cold, Flower' I called, but she laughed and said, 'Don't be silly, Minch. I'm quite all right now. You know that, don't you?'

Sad as I was, the dreams were strangely comforting, for I became all the more certain that we three could never really be separated; that they would keep a place for me, wherever they were. That they would be waiting.

Those dreams began shortly after Dan's death. But, later, the terrible dreams started. I dreamed, once, of them both together. They were thumb-sized foetuses. I had wrapped them in white stuff, a kind of bandage, and put them on the grill plate above the gas hob. There I left them, going away and forgetting them. I was a long way off when I suddenly remembered them but, try as I might, desperate, I couldn't find home. When I got there at last, the foetuses were cold and stiff.

Another time, I dreamed they were sitting next to each other in high chairs and Dan leaned across and held a nappy across Fleur's face as if to smother her. I woke terrified. In another dream – you can never forget them – I heard Fleur calling from the cellar and I ran down to dig her out. I dug her out and took her up and gave her tea, but as soon as I turned my back, she ran back down the cellar steps and disappeared into the sand dunes. Horrific. Horrific: that is all I can say. What was my mind doing? What did the dreams say about me as a mother? I woke guilty, torn and unable to concentrate.

I was probably mad, struggling with the memories, struggling to keep them raw and alive and with me all the time. If I forgot, who could remember? Forgetting is the most punishing thing of all.

Anyway, I don't know why the dreams returned to haunt me just then, but they drove me to make the conscious effort not to think about Guy any more but to concentrate, instead, on Brother Joseph. I could think about him because he was like a child. He needed someone to love him. For him, love was the rabbit, and I was irritated by the idea of the rabbit being put at night into the run, so far from the house. No, I was angry. Something about it all made me angry. I thought it was a kind of bullying. I even considered saying something to Father Godfrey. Can you imagine that? I had only been there five minutes and was thinking of interfering in their business.

I thought about it a lot but in the end decided to be kinder to Joseph, take more trouble with him while I was there. Perhaps, I thought, my time there would not be wasted after all; I could do some good. Why then, after all my good intentions, did my rage get the better of me?

Chapter 31

After leaving the lady, Joseph untied the rabbit and, holding the lead in one hand and dragging the box with the other, stumbled crookedly down the Monks' Walk. The box was awkward, made his fingers ache, and he was obliged to stop every now and again to change hands. All the time he mumbled to his pet, more to comfort himself than anything else, for he was filled with foreboding. 'Tush, tush! All right, Francis. All right.'

Eventually he reached the part where he had to turn to the left and into the overgrown area where the newly renovated run stood.

He hesitated outside the shut gates and then put down the box in order to study the hook and couplet. As if anticipating freedom, the rabbit leapt forwards, taking him by surprise, but he grabbed at the lead, tripping over the box as he did so, and fell heavily onto his side, narrowly missing the rabbit who, jerking forward with fright, took up the slack of the lead and was jolted onto his back.

Joseph lay on the ground hurt and shaken, and, like the rabbit, his body convulsed once or twice as he exhaled. But he never took his eyes off his pet, who righted himself and sat quivering a few yards from him. Slowly, Joseph stretched out his arm along the grass and touched the rabbit on the back. He didn't speak, just hummed in his throat.

Once he had enough breath, he rolled over onto his stomach and then onto his knees. It was difficult to get up from the ground, but, pushing himself up with his one free hand, he manged to wobble onto his feet and straighten slowly.

The box was on its side and the straw had spilled out but there was nothing he could do about that until he had the rabbit safely inside the run. It was a difficult and time-consuming operation undoing the gate with the rabbit in his arms, but eventually he managed to undo the lock and to pull open the gate, which dragged heavily along the thick clumps of grass. It took all the strength he had.

Once inside, he put the animal down and watched as it quivered and sniffed about the edges of the run. 'Come here. Aren't you the wicked one! You rascal, you.'

He leaned against the wire, all his strength gone. He couldn't say how he felt, but he had the same kind of feeling after Billie had died – a kind of fear, a kind of agitation. He looked around at the wire walls, at the trampled grass and weeds. He saw, outside the run, the broken-down wooden kennels where Billie's dogs had slept. Helpless little puppies, soft like Francis and warm. Would the rabbit be warm out here? He had never slept out before, not since he had had him. Would the box be enough? 'Come here Francis! Tush! tush!'

He caught hold of the lead, pulling the rabbit to him. 'Come on,' he whispered, and they left the run and made their way to the graveyard.

The high yew hedge stood at the end of the Monks' Walk, separated by a turnpike gate, which they pushed through and so entered the graveyard. There were the graves either side of a weedy path, at the end of which stood two wooden benches. Joseph sat down and studied the grassy mounds, clothed in tall, tangled grasses. Only Billie's grave was different, for his was worn and flat with Joseph's trimming. Beside the grave was an unused plot marked out with stones. 'That's mine,' he said aloud.

He was perfectly at home, sitting there while flickering moments from the past brought him and Billie together again. All his happiness was linked with Billie. First at the home and then here.

Joseph only knew St Dominic's; he had been there since he was born. He was six when Billie arrived. He was kicking a ball about with some of the others on the old tennis court when Brother James walked out with a new lad. He left him standing alone on the bank overlooking the old court.

Joseph was immediately struck by the boy's white hair and the bruises on the side of his face. The boy did not move or speak, just stood there, and the other boys took no notice of him, but Joseph did. He deliberately kicked the ball up the bank in his direction, to catch his attention, but it rolled back down again without the blond boy understanding the offer of friendship. Joseph made several other attempts at bringing the boy into the game and finally succeeded when the ball hit him on the leg. Then the boy picked it up while all the boys below catcalled and jumped, pushing each other out of the way, each one demanding that the ball be thrown to him. The new boy took his time, as Joseph stood waiting and watching. At last he held the ball high above his head and, eyeing the raging boys below, slowly, thoughtfully tossed the ball to Joseph. The friendship was cemented.

For whatever reason, probably because the brothers recognised Joseph's kind nature, his inability to bully, Billie's bed was put next to his. From this close proximity, they shared secrets: Joseph's beatings for being slow or stupid and his crying in his sleep; Billie's terrors about being 'chosen', his nightmares and bedwetting and, of course, the mouse.

Billie caught a mouse and kept it in a drawer and although Joseph was a chatterbox, frequently speaking without thinking, his lips were firmly sealed when it came to any of Billie's secrets. Billie, in turn, took on a protective role and helped Joseph with his schoolwork, for he was as clever as Joseph was rather dull.

'You're my brother,' Billie said.

'You're mine, too,' Joseph would return, grinning with unreserved delight.

Billie's silence and isolation from all except Joseph contained the shame of an abused child. His mother had neglected him; his father beaten and abused him. It was only after he had been found in the coal-house, beaten and bruised, because a neighbour heard him crying, that he was finally taken into the care of St Dominic's. He never saw his parents again. Joseph was all the family he had and he was all the family Joseph had. Joseph had no family except the brothers – and the boys. But they didn't love him. Only Billie loved him like family.

They left St Dominic's home for St Cuthbert's Abbey together, where they made their vows and Billie took the name of John, although he was always Billie to Joseph.

After seven years, they moved together to Burnham Abbey. Forty-seven years they had together at the abbey before Billie became ill and distracted and fell into complete silence. Even the dogs and the puppies couldn't make him better. He died.

Joseph waded through the fog of reality as he had always done. Accepting. He didn't cry – only in his sleep – but the days were long and grey and he was nervous with emptiness, his energy gone. And then the cat brought in a baby rabbit.

Joseph shuffled down the path to the grave and stood looking down at it. 'Go on, then. Go on then' he mumbled to the rabbit. 'You like it! Yes, you do. For sure, you know!' and then, 'Let's get them, then.'

He pulled the rabbit back to the hedge and, rummaging near the gate, dragged out a pair of shears he'd hidden there. Back to the grave and bending stiffly, he clipped off some longer pieces of grass. It was difficult with the rabbit, but he worked at it for a moment or two and then straightened to look with satisfaction at his work. 'That's better, isn't it?'

But the feeling of agitation wouldn't go away. He waited by

the grave, hoping for the comfort it usually brought him, but the Angelus bell drifted across and he knew he had to leave.

Chapter 32

When I entered the hall on my way to supper, I found Father Godfrey waiting for me.

'Oh dear! Sorry about your foot. How did you do it?'

I told him and he shook his head. 'You must be a very vigorous digger! Be more careful next time.'

'Pretty stupid, wasn't it? Typical, I'm afraid. I do rather go at things like a bull at a gate.' Trying to be flippant, making a joke.

'Well, you're in good hands, at any rate, so come and enjoy your supper.'

He put out his hand to usher me forward.

'We're very lucky, very lucky indeed to have Brother Guy to look after all our little aches and pains. We shall be sorry to lose him.'

I know I stopped for a moment. 'Is he going somewhere, then?' But he continued on into the refectory and didn't seem to hear.

I was getting used to the silent meals and the bland faces and less shy about looking around. I could study them as they ate, for they seldom took their eyes off their plates. A large, puffy-faced, bald-headed man was reading that evening. He read in a slow, singsong fashion, enunciating his words as if he were spitting out cherry stones. I thought him pompous. Joseph was bent double over his plate as he sorted through his food and when I caught his eye, he ignored my smile. I was a bit hurt, actually. I thought we were kind of friends. The spotty youth was sitting next to him, but I couldn't look because I knew I would feel sick. His good-looking companion who had helped find the spade was on the top table and I wondered how the places were chosen. Did every place have a special meaning and, if so, what meaning could be attached to mine? A place for the mad, perhaps. I tried to avoid looking at Guy, but somehow he looked over and raised his eyebrows, intimately I thought, asking about my foot. I gave a slight shrug and went back to my salad, but I could feel myself blushing.

After supper, he waited for me outside and smiled broadly when he saw me. He seemed so relaxed and I felt so tense. I don't know why.

'How is it?' he asked

'OK.'

'Still hurting badly?'

'No – it's better.'

'Good. Well, come on, then. Let's get it over with.'

I wasn't sure what that meant. Did he want to get rid of the task, get rid of me? I decided I wouldn't take one more minute of his time than absolutely necessary.

I sat on the chair as before and again he pulled up his chair close to me. He pulled off my shoe, which was so tight around the swelling that it had cut a deep red trench into the puffy skin.

He laughed. 'The shoe's doing more damage than the fork. Haven't you got anything better than these sandals? You must have slippers.'

'No, nothing. Nothing here. I travelled light.'

He lifted my foot and examined the marks and the swelling, prodding really gently. 'Sorry! But this won't do. I think I'll have to lend you mine. This foot's so swollen it should fit my slippers perfectly.'

'Slippers? I don't need them both.'

'One's no good to me. Might as well have them both for the time being, until we can get that swelling down.'

He undid the dressing and tossed it into a pedal bin under the table. He had nice hands. Long-fingered and sensitive. Mine, I thought, were rough in comparison and my nails chipped in places. Probably bitten down. My foot was blackish-blue, but the bleeding had stopped and the hole now looked rather insignificant.

'I think we need to put on some ice,' he said. 'I'll get some from the kitchen. Won't be a minute.'

I just sat there. It was quiet without him, just the battery clock on the wall faintly clicking. I wished I could be relaxed like him. Why couldn't I be easy and laid-back and cheerful? Really cheerful, not pretending all the time. I wanted to be easy. I wanted to accept his kindness and his care. But I was afraid. Had I always been this complicated? Difficult, my mother used to say. I was brought up to believe that in some way I was difficult, although I was never sure in what way. Outspoken? A bit too direct? Stubborn? Is that being difficult? Peter didn't think I was difficult, until the end, of course. Or perhaps he did and never said. Perhaps people have never said. And the children? Surely not. Surely they didn't find me difficult.

Was Guy's cheerfulness because he knew my story? I guessed Father Godfrey had filled him in. So Guy was especially kind and caring not because of me, Rose, me the person, but because of what had happened. That was all.

He came back with a pudding basin filled with ice cubes and a tea towel over his arm. He gave me the bowl. 'Hold some on for as long as you can. Look, here's a tea towel.'

He took back the bowl and wrapped ice cubes into the cotton tea towel, knotting it from corner to corner.

'Stop some of the drips.'

Gosh, the cold on my foot was painful! But I held it like a brave child, like the brave child I had been with my father, so he would be proud of me.

Meanwhile, Guy fetched more bandages and cream from the cupboard.

'Where are you going?' I didn't know I was going to ask; I just asked. 'Father Godfrey told me you were leaving here.'

'Did he, now?'

'Yes. Do you mind my asking?'

'I think that will do,' he said, as if to change the subject, and took away the bowl and began wiping my foot dry with some lint before putting on the cream. All the time he had my foot on his knee. I was very conscious of that. He rebandaged it and put my foot down.

'I'm going back into general practice. Does that meet with your approval?' He laughed again.

I said it wasn't really for me to approve or disapprove; it was up to him, but why did he come in the first place?

He told me he had found general practice rather frustrating at times, and was disappointed with what he could achieve. He was amazingly honest, I thought; it couldn't have been easy for him to say all that.

'It's bad enough with the older patients, but with the chil—' And he stopped.

So then I knew he knew. He wasn't laughing and he looked away from me for the first time.

He picked up a roll of sticky tape and fastened the bandage.

'So, you gave up?' It was an unkind challenge. Completely unnecessary, I see that now, but I could hear Fleur with hands on her hips. 'Don't give up, Minch, don't give up.'

He didn't answer and I thought, I've blown it. I've gone too far again. That's it. Why should he bother with me now?

But suddenly he turned in his chair, arms folded. 'You can call it that if you, like,' he said. 'Some people would undoubtedly think so.'

His mouth tightened and his lips had a kind of tremble. Was he angry? Somehow, I was afraid of his change of mood; it made me want to cry, but I didn't. I persisted but more gently. I spoke softly; I know I did.

'Did you come here because you are religious, then? Rather

than, say, go overseas to Africa, for instance, where it seems good doctors are so badly needed? Just wondering.'

'Life is not quite as simple as that.'

I could see he was uncomfortable so why did I go on?

But he did answer, sort of. He just said something like, 'You're right, I could have gone to work abroad, but there are many questions to try to answer and I decided I might find some answers here.'

'And did you?'

I was so pleased when he laughed again, but he turned away and said. 'Well, let's put it like this: I'm learning to accept my limitations.' Adding with another laugh, 'And there are quite a lot!'

He had been almost a year at the abbey, he said.

'Tell me,' I asked, 'honestly, do you think all this prayer business does any good at all? Or is it a complete waste of time? I mean God, or whatever it is, doesn't answer prayer. Doesn't bring rain to drought-ridden places, didn't protect those terribly abused children in Romania. Oh, my God, how awful was that? And we all prayed and prayed. Bloody useless.'

He waited, his arms folded while I exploded. So childish. But I could see in his eyes that he knew I was thinking about my kids. About myself. All the anger directed somewhere else. And he was a doctor and I needed help.

He had finished tidying up, finished turning away, and sat quite purposefully in his chair, facing me.

'As a matter of fact, I do think prayers, meditation, just thinking sometimes, can work, but not at all in the way we hope. I don't think God can stop wars or make the sick well, the sorts of things we all want.'

He was beginning to make me angry again. He was not saying what I wanted to hear.

'So, you do think whatever's out there is powerless, then? Or not there at all, of course. What do you honestly think, because I think that, whatever it is, it's powerless. It's taken me all this time to understand how conned we were as children, conned by the Bible stories, just as we were conned by the 'happy ever after' fairy stories. Cinderella did not go to the ball; she spent the rest of her life as a drudge, doing the cleaning and whatever. It was the ugly sisters who went to the ball and ended up marrying lords and princes. The frog prince remains a frog and the ugly duckling was pecked to death.'

His face! I couldn't help bursting out with laughter. And he laughed, too. We both laughed.

'I'm afraid, Guy, faith never, ever moved mountains. It really is the most awful load of cobblers.'

'In that way, I am sure you're right,' he said. 'But—'

I interrupted him: 'But isn't it depressing, this powerlessness? Powerlessness is the most awful thing. I can understand how you feel when you can't make someone better. I really do.'

There were some footsteps and low voices outside, so he leaned forward to speak.

'The thing is,' he said. 'I think it's the ideas, you see. It's called inspiration. In spirit, you see. But we have to make them work, the ideas. It's up to us in the end.'

'Up to us what?' I was getting angry again.

He hesitated. 'To do our best, I suppose. Just to do our best. Simple as that.'

The noise outside had faded. We didn't need to speak quietly any more.

'Simple as that!' I repeated. Inside was a small edge of relief that I didn't recognise at the time. Just that I felt less battered.

'The problem is,' he was saying, although I was hardly listening, 'that we know so little still, so very little, and we can't do what we don't know. It's not our fault, of course – shouldn't beat ourselves up about it, because it's like expecting a young child to be able to understand higher maths or argue about philosophy. They can't because they're not ready. Might well be able to when grown up, though, if you see what I mean.'

I was beginning to see what he meant. I've thought about it a lot since.

'But there is this hope, you know. After all, many people are living healthy lives who, years ago, would be dead. In the meantime, I share your frustrations.'

'So, we're alone?'

'No, not at all. Look, we have each other.'

But it wasn't enough for me and it was patronising and a platitude. I wanted anger then, and a kind of revenge.

We still hadn't spoken about the children. Why was he deliberately avoiding it? He was the doctor, after all, and I was the patient. I had come here to find some kind of healing. He didn't mention my memory problems. Damn him, I thought.

And then out of the blue he said, 'Oh, by the way, changing the subject completely, would you like a day out tomorrow? I think it would do you good. No walking, just a ride in the car to fetch stuff from the farm and, well, we could even treat ourselves to a cream tea. Would you like that? After all, you can't do any more gardening!' He laughed.

Of course I would like it. I tried not to look too pleased, but suddenly felt a flicker of joy, happy that he had asked. I liked him. I thought he could really put me right and be there for me. I had felt so lonely for such a long time.

'That would be nice,' I said.

'Good!' He was quite matter-of-fact. 'Ten o'clock outside the front. OK?'

'OK.'

Chapter 33

As we walked down the corridor towards the central lobby, he having insisted that he would walk with me back to my room, saying that he wanted a breath of fresh air, we saw the rabbit hopping about on the end of the lead. Brother Joseph was wedged in the half-shut kitchen door, on the one hand allowing himself the company of those brothers still in the kitchen and on the other hand keeping an eye out for me, it seemed. The rabbit he was obediently restraining from entering the kitchen and so he had his arm extended out as if, in some strange way, he was directing traffic.

As soon as he saw us approaching, he leapt into the corridor, grinning in expectation.

'We've been waiting for you,' he said.

I tried to look pleased.

'Mrs Gregory's going back to her room now,' Guy said rather too firmly, and he pushed me forward.

'She's said she'd help me settle Francis for the night, didn't you?' His breath rose hot and sour into my face.

'I don't think Mrs Gregory should do any walking tonight, Brother. I'll come with you.'

Joseph's face fell and he turned abruptly, mumbling.

'I think I did say something,' I whispered. 'I won't go far – I'll take care.'

'Well, it's not with my approval,' he said rather sternly, and I laughed as he shook his head in mock despair.

'I did promise.'

'Right! See you tomorrow, then, for the drive out.'

'Yes.'

Joseph was shuffling slowly down the corridor, clearly hoping that I would catch him up, which I did.

'Like to hold the lead?'

Outside it was warm and night was falling. The grass was already damp, and far away across the trees a pair of owls screeched back and forth.

I could never have found my way alone, for everything seemed quite different now in the dusk, but I was aware of the long grasses and several times spreading brambles caught the edges of my skirt. The overhanging beech trees, dark and still, blocked out the light and bushes took on a rounded solidity, each appearing from out of the dimness unexpectedly. It was even difficult to make out the rabbit at times, as his mottled fur merged with the blotchy shadows. Only his eyes caught some rare light every so often and sparked intermittently.

I heard Brother Joseph softly panting as he led the way along the avenue and towards the yet unexplored wilderness.

After some time, the trees opened out and the path forked; here Joseph veered towards the left, disappearing from view, leaving the rabbit with me. I could just hear him muttering to himself, then a rattling sound and then silence.

I know I called out because I was nervous, 'Brother Joseph, I can't see you.'

He emerged from the darkness as quickly as he had disappeared. 'Over here,' he said, and took the lead out of my hand.

I followed as quickly as my aching foot would allow and around the corner I saw the dog run. It stood faint and insubstantial, a large wire structure supported by thin wood slats. The wire door, framed with wood, stood crookedly open, its bottom hidden amongst thick clumps of rough grass.

Joseph dragged the rabbit through the door and made towards something, which turned out to be a large cardboard box. I pushed the gate closed. Joseph was bending over the box, shuffling his hand backwards and forwards inside it. When I looked, I saw straw in the bottom.

'He's used to this,' he said, and bent to pick up his rabbit. 'It's your bed, isn't it, Francis?' He turned to me. 'He used to this,' – indicating the box – 'but I don't think he'll like it out here. It's only what they want.' He fondled the rabbit in his arms. 'But it's not what we want, is it, Francis?'

I ruffled my hand on the rabbit's head and my hand brushed against the rough, brittle skin of the old man. It contrasted sharply with the soft fur and I suddenly felt depressed and irritable. Why were they doing this to him?

But I said, 'I'm sure he will be really OK here. He'll be warm and snug and it's probably better for him than being inside all night. Don't you think?'

'It's the foxes, though. The foxes get about at night. They do, indeed.'

'Foxes?'

'First a cat and now a fox.'

I wasn't feeling well and my foot was hurting; it had been stupid of me to go, but I did kind of wander around the run, trying to inspect the structure more closely. It seemed safe enough. The wire was, I guessed, six feet high. Surely nothing could get over that. But I was angry. Perhaps I was angry because I didn't want to bother with it all; I didn't want to care. I didn't have the energy to care.

'I think it's perfectly safe. Don't worry. Shall we put him in now?' It wasn't just that my foot was aching badly, nor that the damp was somehow chilling me; it was because I thought the sooner it was done, the better.

'Come on, Francis. Let's put you to bed now.'

He bent and dropped the rabbit into the box and it scratched and twisted, turning wildly several times. Joseph giggled. 'He always does that.' And then he fished in his pockets and took out a carrot and some quarters of apple. 'Here you are.'

The rabbit eyed us both in the dark, his ears on the alert and his nose quivering and, apparently forgetting us completely, began sniffing at the food. We watched for a moment and then I took Joseph's arm and led him out of the run.

I made myself do it. It wasn't easy, because in some ways he disgusted me, but I did continue with my arm through his. He held his arm limply by his side, giving no sign that I was there at all, quite engrossed in his own thoughts, but I sensed that he didn't mind. I tried to think of something to say to break the silence; it was like dealing with a sorrowing child.

'Can you imagine why I'm here? So stupid, really!'

No reply.

'It's really so silly. Shall I tell you?' And I gave a light laugh so as to make a joke out of it, but he failed to respond. 'The thing is, for some extraordinary reason, I started losing my memory. At work, mostly. Silly things. I suddenly couldn't spell simple words, forgot words, things like that – sometimes I couldn't understand what I was reading. You know I would look at loads of change in my purse and couldn't work out how much it was. Not all the time, just sometimes. Mind went blank – felt like cotton wool. Awful! And then I panicked and that made it worse. A bit like looking at an exam question and thinking that it was double Dutch. Thinking, I don't know what they're talking about. Not too good, don't you think?' I tried to laugh again, tried to take his mind off the rabbit.

Silence.

'The thing is…' I began to tell him about the children. Things I had never spoken of before: about the drive in the car; about the red blanket and the little strand of hair across Fleur's face; about Dan and the boat and my cowardice; about the tubes and the machines. About Peter. I was unemotional, as if I was telling a bedtime story. A story about somebody else. How I couldn't remember Fleur's funeral; how I couldn't remember what they liked to eat; how I couldn't remember how much I loved them.

I turned to look at him, his face pale in the shadowy dark and, as I did so, he pulled away, leaned over the path and vomited in great streams, down his clothes, into his hands, onto the grass.

Christ! I jumped away, horrified, my stomach retching with his. But at least I did not run away. I pulled up clumps of grass for him to wipe himself with.

'What's the matter? What's wrong?' I was sure it must be something I had said. Perhaps all of it. Perhaps it was too much. 'What's wrong?' I asked again, but he was rubbing down his habit with a grubby handkerchief. I pushed some grass into his hands, thinking he could wipe himself with it, but he looked at me questioningly and then let it drop onto the path. I felt so ashamed. Had I been the cause?

'Is it Francis? Is that what's upset you?' but he was already shuffling away from me, rather bent, his head down. I felt a rush of fury. I would most definitely go to see Father Godfrey. I watched him stumbling on into the weak, low light of the evening, which spread through the widening trees at the end of the path. I did not hurry to catch him up and although unsure that it had not been me that had upset him, I turned on impulse, deciding that I would go to see Father Godfrey at once.

There was absolutely no one in the hallway, but I knew his room was somewhere through the door to the right and, determined now to do what I had come to do, I opened the door and passed through. Beyond the library was another door and a light shone underneath. I supposed it was Godfrey's. Perhaps in some strange way it was the thought of my trip out the next morning, for I was looking forward to it, that meant I felt no qualms in knocking on this door. I heard the scrape of a chair and almost immediately the door opened. Godfrey was standing there.

'I'm sorry to disturb you, but I think you ought to know that Brother Joseph is ill. He's just been horribly sick. And I'm sure it's because of the rabbit.' I know I rattled on something like: 'He's very upset, you know, about putting the rabbit in that run. I thought you'd like to know.'

He just stared at me.

'Well, that's all I came to say. Goodnight.'

I knew I'd been rude, but I didn't care. His silence only increased my irritation. He was about to shut the door without a word when I turned.

'I think it's all pretty disgraceful,' I kind of shouted, and strode off, leaving him standing there. I don't quite know what came over me. I didn't have to be so aggressive, did I?

As I crossed the lawn, still shaking from my outburst, I saw two monks entering the Monks' Walk. As it was almost dark, I couldn't make out exactly who they were, but I was surprised and curious, so I stood where I was, not wanting to attract attention. They were speaking quietly and soon disappeared into the trees, at which point, in my curiosity, I walked quickly to the path that led to my room, from where I could watch them.

One was the rather fat bald-headed monk. I recognised him from behind for, every now and again, in the near dark, the filtered light caught the top of his bald, skull-like head. The smaller, rather quick-stepped monk I couldn't place at all. But as I watched, I saw them stretch out their hands to each other. I stared, mesmerised; couldn't believe what I was seeing. Then they both stopped, turned towards each other, pulled their hoods up over their heads and kissed. I shouldn't have been so shocked, I suppose, but I was and it just added to my anxiety; that this abbey was not the place for me; that the whole idea had been a really stupid mistake. Where were Matthew, or Seamus or Peter, Mother, Father? All gone from me, one way or the other.

Chapter 34

Godfrey was so amazed at the woman's behaviour that he immediately shut his door to hide his consternation, and poured himself out a sherry. The music had stopped and he sat in the silence with the glass in his hand. He was bemused and thoroughly shaken. He had thought her so calm, so perfectly in control; he had been drawn to her and yet there she had stood like something demented. At one point, he had honestly thought she was going to strike him.

He passed a hand over his head, gulped some sherry and tried in his mind to account for her behaviour, even to make excuses for her. Even if she were right, that was no way to behave, bursting in on him like that and leave him standing there like an idiot. It was all too much. How were they to cope? He had too much on his plate at the moment; he just could not tolerate anything more. The man from the auction house was coming tomorrow, too. And then he remembered that Guy was taking her out. Thank goodness for that! Keep her out of the way for as long as possible. He would have a word with Guy first thing tomorrow. Perhaps he could persuade her to go home, even. It was a doctor she needed, not a priest. And then he remembered Guy was a doctor. He sighed in exasperation. It didn't seem to matter which way he turned, something or someone was snapping at his heels.

He pushed himself up from his chair, tired and depressed. He felt extraordinarily helpless, but he supposed he should go to see if Brother Joseph was all right. She was bound to ask, and to find out that he didn't go … then there would be another scene. Damn the woman! He couldn't help himself. All because of a stupid rabbit! He couldn't believe anything so trivial could cause so much fuss. And damn Bertram, too!

When he reached Joseph's room, there was no sign of life. He knocked very gently on his door, praying that there would be no answer, and there wasn't. He sighed quietly with relief and then hesitated. Perhaps he was too ill to answer! He knocked again. Nothing. Suddenly he was consumed by tiredness. I can't do any more, he thought and so returned to his room, longing for the oblivion of sleep.

Chapter 35

There was the echo of a cuckoo, its hollow call of dewy sunshine and bluebell woods, and I lay listening, aware of a quickening, a lightness. I was going out with Guy. I didn't want to lie in bed, but it was much too early to do anything. And then I thought of the rabbit. I would go and see it, see that it had survived the night. I was glad to have a purpose; I was energised for the first time in goodness knows how long! My foot still throbbed a bit, but I didn't care.

I put on the kettle and lit a cigarette, which I puffed at as I dressed. The milk was off and I opened the door and threw it into the shrubs; it left white drops on the thick leaves. The sun was just appearing through the trees, casting long fingers of light. It was going to be another scorcher and I think I was almost happy, although I did wonder with a wry twist whether I would dare go to breakfast after last night's debacle with Father Godfrey, but decided that I most definitely would; they didn't take any notice of me, anyway. So what would be different about this morning?

I remembered the two holding hands. Could I identify the smaller of the two at breakfast? My shock had turned to amusement; I didn't care about it or them any more. It was my secret, although I would tell Guy. I thought we could have a laugh about it.

In the meantime, as I had time, I would go and check on the rabbit, but as I came to the end of my path and in sight of the great cedar tree I was surprised and kind of relieved to see the rabbit already tied to the rope.

Momentarily I was at a bit of a loss, with no reason to go for the walk to check him out, and unsure what to do. I was up early, but nevertheless, anyone could be looking at me from out of a window somewhere, so trying, rather self-consciously, to look as if I knew what I was doing, I walked over to the rabbit as purposefully as I could, bent down to touch his ears and kicked some scraps in his direction.

Joseph was nowhere to be seen; no one was around. It was so still, so silent, I could hear the rabbit's quivering and soft hoppings.

'You've survived all right, then? I shouted at Father Godfrey about you out there. Do you realise? But you were OK after all. I think I must be silly, Francis.'

Later, at breakfast, I looked defiantly round but they all, even Father Godfrey, stared resolutely at their plates, deliberately avoiding me. Except for Guy. We looked across at each other and he winked. Why did that scare me? Why did I suddenly not want to go out with him? I was a grown woman behaving like a teenager, for God's sake.

I left the dining room before him, hoping to get out of the building before he caught up with me, which I felt sure he would try to do. And I was right for, as I went to open the French windows, I heard his voice.

'How are you this morning?'

'Fine!'

'The foot more comfortable? I see you have abandoned my slippers!'

'Better, thank you.' I ignored the reference to the slippers. Too personal.

'Ready for the outing, then?'

'Yep.'

'Good. Well, I should be ready by ten-thirty. See you out at the front. Don't wear anything too grand.' His voice was full of laughter.

'We're going to a farm, remember!'

But I was already crossing by the tree and pretended not to hear.

Chapter 36

He had his back to me and was putting something into his car, which he had driven up beside mine. He was wearing fawn corduroys and a white shirt with the sleeves half rolled up. He turned when he heard me and, looking happy, opened his arms in greeting, smiling broadly.

'I didn't recognise you.' And he laughed. He seemed so very pleased to see me. And it made me happy. It was something I wasn't used to, had forgotten about. And I think he knew it.

'All ready? Good. Well, get in.'

He opened the passenger door for me and pushed the sleeve of my jumper, which was hanging over my shoulders, safely out of the way before shutting the door. Nobody had taken care of me like that for such a long time. And to be taken out! To be driven, not having to find my way alone. I wanted to hug him. Of course, I did nothing of the sort.

It was a small car, rather grubby inside and the back seat was piled up with empty egg cartons and wooden fruit boxes.

'It's a bit of a wreck, isn't it?' he said as he squeezed his long legs under the steering wheel; he looked uncomfortable. 'An old dear in the parish left it to the abbey. But it goes all right. I give it a going-over every so often. As a matter of fact, I gave it a clean yesterday, believe or not, especially for you!'

'Really?'

'Thanks very much!'

And I laughed at his easy manner, his understanding of my strange humour. Not everybody did.

'You're good at cars, are you?' I asked.

'I wouldn't say that. But it's in my own interests.'

He kept turning his head to look at me. I looked straight ahead as if I hadn't noticed.

'I'm the only one who can drive here, so I get to use it. And believe me, I'll find every excuse!'

He had backed the car into the lane, which it seemed I'd driven up years ago. The overhanging beeches cast dark patches across the cracked and pitted surface, and the shadows deepened and lightened like waves as the sun moved in and out of the clouds, for the day, though very warm, had produced some clouds, which moved heavy and ponderously, so there were moments of bright heat followed by a duller humidity.

I wound down the window and the wind caught the top of my head, blowing my hair about. He nodded in mutual enjoyment and somehow, I knew that there had been no need to ask if he minded the window open. Then he pressed in a cassette and we travelled in silence for quite some time and the music, crackling every now and then, was the excuse. He was so easy, so undemanding that I wanted to cry. But I never cried, remember, and so I fumbled in my shoulder bag, firstly finding a handkerchief and then my dark glasses. To hide what? Nothing. Guy turned momentarily towards me. I'm not sure if he knew or not, but he said nothing.

We were travelling along the tree-lined lane that led away from the abbey. In between the trees were wheat fields, meadowland, farmhouses and odd cottages surrounded by barns and tractors. Clumps of distant trees sheltered horses from the sun and just for a second I saw the glint of water.

'Is there a river anywhere round here? I am quite besotted by rivers.'

'Yes, we can find a river, but it means walking a bit. What about your foot?'

He turned quickly to look at me and I caught his eyes for a moment.

'It's much better. Anyway, I wouldn't let it stop me from going to a river.' As I imagined the river – it sounds mad I know – but I longed to be submerged in the water, to feel it, cool and cleansing. I wanted it to ripple across my eyes and forehead, easing the tension and anxiety.

'I would really like to find a river.'

'I think we should do whatever we want, whenever we can, don't you?'

'So that's your philosophy, is it?'

'Definitely!'.

'Could be a bit dangerous, couldn't it?'

'Perhaps.'

I noticed that awful seriousness come over his face, the look I had seen before, and it unnerved me. It was the look of someone who has something dreadful to tell. What was it he knew that he was going to have to tell me? All the terror and panics of days in the past caused my skin to quiver. Then he laughed. And I wanted to laugh too, but instead I looked out of the window.

'Well, I'll take you to a river. Before or after lunch?'

'Lunch?'

'Oh, yes. We're going out to lunch.'

'That's nice. I don't mind. Perhaps before.'

We came to a T-junction and turned left into a main road.

'Nearly there,' he said. 'Now this is a real farm if ever there was one. Animals, vegetables, flowers – the lot.' And almost at once we turned, again to the left, through wooden five-barred gates, which stood wedged in baked mud tracks and tied back with barbed wire.

The track, lying between potato fields, wound gently round to the right, where stood two dilapidated outbuildings, two tractors, piles of old car tyres and rusty corrugated iron, which lay haphazardly amongst long grass. Some polythene covering hung limply across the entrance to the buildings; it looked more like a scrapyard than a farm.

The farmhouse only came into view as we continued rounding the bend. It lay several yards beyond and behind the outbuildings. It was a small, red-bricked Victorian house with tall chimneys and a green wooden porch badly in need of fresh paint. Some geraniums in pots stood on the ground outside the porch, perhaps ready for someone to collect.

Guy drove round the side of the house and parked the car beside an old oak tree from which two thick ropes hung from what must have been a treehouse, although the planks were rotting and broken.

'Coming?'

'No, you go. I'll stay here.'

He held up a hand. 'Won't be long.'

He opened the boot and took out the piles of egg boxes and disappeared somewhere behind the back of the house.

I was drawn to the oak tree because in my mind I could see the pigeon, caught by its ringed leg, hanging upside down from one of the branches of the old pear tree in our garden. I heard again Fleur's heartfelt sobs and felt her hand banging on my thigh. 'Do something, Mummy. Oh, do something quickly. Poor little thing.'

I had wanted to laugh at her ferociousness, but she banged me again. It was no use: I obviously had to do something and so I went next door to Josephine, who came with Jill trailing behind her and all three of us stood beneath the tree and studied the bird, which hung limply, while Fleur, who had retreated upstairs to get a better view, banged on the glass and cried from her bedroom window.

The bird looked absurd hanging there, caught by the ring on one foot, and we all, rather cruelly, wanted to laugh, but a further glance at Fleur's tear-stained face pressed against the bedroom window soon wiped the instinctive smiles from our faces.

'Call the fire brigade,' Jill had demanded, and so we did. Much to my embarrassment, a fire engine arrived and two firemen jumped from the cab.

'In the back.' Jill pointed, and so up the garden path, through the side gate and into the garden they tramped.

Once under the tree they stared, bewildered, at the hanging pigeon. I had expected them to use ladders at least – it was the only reason I had called them – but no, instead the larger of the two men wedged himself into the lower branches and instructed his smaller, rather frail companion. It was like a Laurel and Hardy episode, so ridiculous. I thought the smaller man would never manage to steady himself on his companion's shoulders and meanwhile the one underneath was red in the face, increasingly bending and puffing; I really thought he would have a heart attack, but eventually the little fireman (Laurel!) did succeed in half standing on the shoulders of the large man (Hardy!) wobbling underneath. But he couldn't reach the pigeon.

'Pass us a stick up,' he panted to me, while I stood staring at the whole procedure with utter incredulity. I picked up a fallen twig from the lawn and handed it up, and with this the by now hot and flustered man hit out frantically in all directions at the terrified pigeon, all the time obeying the grunting, painful commands from the crumpling shoulders below.

Suddenly, and unexpectedly the pigeon was loose. It dropped like a stone, recovered for an instant, flapped a couple of times and then dived over the hedge and dropped quite dead onto Josephine's lawn.

Oh my God. I had to lie to Fleur, who couldn't have seen the pigeon's final descent. 'The pigeon's fine, Flower,' I lied to the tear-stained and anxious face.' He's flown back to his nest now, I should think. Isn't that a good thing? Good thing you made me do something.'

I did lie over things like that. If the cat caught a mouse, or worse still a bird, Fleur screamed to *do something* and every time I would lie that everything was OK, that I had rescued whatever it was that needed rescuing, otherwise the tears and sobbing would have been too awful.

I was so happy to have remembered that. It didn't make me cry, which was just as well, as round from the back came a small, wiry woman with short-cropped grey hair, wearing baggy blue trousers and a navy-blue-and-white T-shirt. She was carrying a wooden box. She crossed behind the tree and went into a shed, reappearing a moment later with what looked like a box filled with cabbages. 'It must be some sort of garden shop,' I thought. She returned without a glance in my direction and again I heard voices and laughter. The woman and Guy? I couldn't be sure, but honestly, I think for moment I was jealous because they had a relationship, knew each other in a way that excluded me. I was the outsider. I didn't know them and they didn't know me. But they knew each other and would do long after I had disappeared from the scene, and I wished I wasn't there at all. The truth is difficult sometimes.

I sat in the car feeling isolated, but I did give myself a talking-to – I think out loud (first sign of madness): 'Make an effort. Get out and be sociable.'

But I left the car door open, wishing, as it were, to hedge my bets; I could always return quickly and no one would be any the wiser. The voices were further off. Would it seem like an intrusion? I didn't know what to do, couldn't make up my mind whether to go on or whether to return to the car.

It was always the same; I could never make up my mind about anything. Over the simplest choices, I would be in confusion: what to wear; what to eat; what to do. The only release was to go to bed and sleep and then I didn't have to think about anything for an hour or two. Except I hadn't slept properly for so long I had forgotten what a good, deep, restful sleep was. It was a miracle that I had managed to work and even more that I had managed to get myself to the abbey, but then, I had had no real choice. It had been that or hospital, for 'a thorough rest', the doctor had said.

Guy appeared around the corner.

'Oh, there you are. I was coming to fetch you. Do come and see the chicks.'

I went with him round the back of the farm and into the open garden, which was mainly a rough, bumpy lawn surrounded with wide herbaceous borders. The bottom of the garden led naturally into the farm, only separated from it by a worn footpath, which ran along the bottom. We followed this and I could hear the frantic cheeping before I saw the masses of yellow chicks. We stopped by the wired pen and watched the heaving, jostling yellow fluff peep and push and peck. I glanced up at Guy, who was grinning at me. 'Sweet?' he questioned.

'Yes!'

'I thought you'd like them.'

There was something about the chicks that reminded me of the rabbit and Brother Joseph. 'There's something I want to talk to you about. About Brother Joseph.'

'When we've finished what we're doing. You stay here if you want while I just pile the stuff into the car.'

I watched him go round the back of the house, outside of which stood laden vegetable boxes, and I assumed he was going for those, but he emerged carrying the filled egg cartons. I indicated did he need help, but he shook his head.

'Stay there,' he shouted as he rounded the corner to the car. 'Molly wants a word with you.'

I looked round, expecting to see someone, but there was no one about. I heard the car boot bang shut and hoped that Guy would return before I had to face 'Molly' on my own. He returned beaming and rubbing some earth off his hands.

'Everything done,' he said. 'Molly not appeared yet? Well, come on, she's over there.' And he pointed to a greenhouse a couple of hundred yards to the right.

'Who's Molly?'

'There she is!' And the woman I had seen earlier hurried towards us carrying a large pink geranium.

'I had to plant it up,' she said somewhat breathlessly. 'It's called "Florentine".' She held it out to me. 'Might take a day or two to settle. You can keep it in the pot or put it in the ground. Whatever you want. But give it a drop more water when you get back.'

' For me or…?' I looked from the geranium in the woman's hands to Guy, but he had turned away and was stroking one of the farm cats as it lay in the grass that bordered the path.

'You can choose another colour if you prefer, but I thought you would like this best.' She spoke with familiarity, as if she'd known and liked me for years, as if I belonged quite naturally, like everything else in her life. There was a selflessness about her, a practical, useful energy. I couldn't imagine her worrying about tomorrow. She would be too busy just living life as it came. No amount of philosophy or introspection would alter, after all, the movement of the sun, of night or day, the seasons in their time. One was part of it and that was all. Take no thought for tomorrow, or yesterday. Sufficient unto today. Perhaps that's what we should always do. Live today as if there had been no yesterday and will be no tomorrow. Memory's the problem.

'It's really lovely. Thank you. It will look beautiful in one of the pots outside my house.'

'Well, there you are then.' Still holding it, she led the way back to the car, turning all the time to talk.

She handed the pot to me once I'd settled back into the car – there was no room anywhere else – and then stood for a moment speaking to Guy before he, too, got in. She waved goodbye before hurrying behind the house. He hooted goodbye as we drove away.

'Right! Now let's find that river, shall we?'

Chapter 37

The air was now humid under the thickening purple clouds, which graduated in darkness as they glided away from the choked sunlight. Guy opened his window but even the draught was clammy and airless. I sat still, clutching the plant and gazing out the window, and I felt happy and as comfortable as possible for me at that time, but there was this thing, this stuff not talked about that got in the way. And I knew he would never speak of it first. I just knew it. And I thought, It's today or never.

'Did you know both my children died?'

'Yes. I'm sorry.'

'How? Father Godfrey?'

'Yes, I want to—'

'That's why I'm here, I suppose, in a roundabout way. Going a bit crackers, I suppose.'

Guy made to pull the car off the road, but I didn't want to face him then, to be intimate in any way.

'Don't stop.'

He turned the car back to the road and with him driving along, his eyes on the road, I was able to tell him everything. Telling Brother Joseph the night before had been a kind of rehearsal. I was matter-of-fact, and he listened and we both looked straight ahead. I didn't cry. 'So, that's it,' I concluded. 'There's nothing more to say, really. So, don't worry. Don't be concerned. It's not as if I'm the only one. Sadness is not my prerogative, so let's just go on having a nice day. And let's find that river.'

I threw him a bright half-smile. Anything to appear brave, not self-pitying. Did he ever realise what a mask I wore?

He said nothing immediately, but I could almost hear him thinking what to say. It was like a ticking clock.

'What you've been through is horrendous, Rose. Beyond imagination. You are right, there are no words.'

'That's OK. I don't really feel anything, so don't feel sad for me – or whatever you might feel. My mouth speaks, but my heart feels nothing. I'm not sad, I'm just a bit – well, blank, I suppose.'

He shook his head. 'Of course you're sad. You seem devastated to me. '

'Do I? Well, I suppose that's good in a way. Shows I feel something.'

He ignored all my stupid quips and looked a bit helpless.

'Don't let's talk about it any more. I'm enjoying today. Thank you for today. And it's so nice to be driven, be in the passenger seat for once.'

'Well, today is not over yet. Lots more surprises!' And the laugh, the warmth returned to his voice. There was something about that, something about him. He was so easy, so comfortable to be with. It was such a relief, like a soothing drug to a pain-ridden body.

'What then? What surprises?'

'Wait and see.'

Now he turned the car into a narrow lane edged with wide, unkempt grass verges, smothered in white cow parsley and dandelions, straggly briar and hawthorn hedges heavy with overripe and falling white blossoms, and pulled onto the grass opposite a public footpath and stile. Beyond this lay clumpy fields of grass, shaded by clusters of oak trees, which sloped down to the river. Because it was so heavy and overcast there was none of the filtering sunlight and shadows, which I particularly loved; the water alone lit up the humid gloom.

‘There’s your river!’

‘Fantastic!’

‘Do you think you can walk that far?’ He noticed my sandals and where I had cut the strap that ran across the bandage.

I nodded.

‘Careful, then.’

He held out his hand for me as I climbed over the stile, but I managed on my own, deliberately.

‘OK? Well done.’ He offered his arm for some support.

I was suddenly unreasonably excited. ‘You know what? I really wish we could see … some kingcups.’ Then just for a moment I took his arm. ‘They remind me of my childhood. I’m always searching for kingcups. There’s something about them. Don’t you think?”

‘I don’t quite know about those,’ he said, ‘but you’ll find plenty of watercress, if that will do.’

‘Not quite the same!’ We laughed and I let go of his arm and moved off towards the water. It was only yards away.

‘I’m going to paddle! Good for my foot, doctor.’

The river, more of a stream really, was only a few feet across, shallow and clear. The water splashed refreshingly in the breathless air and rocked fronds of green weed back and forth. And he was right: there were thick shining clumps of watercress, the dark, round leaves sky-lit with water drops. I really wanted to paddle.

I took off my sandals and, holding them in my hands, stepped carefully down the shallow bank and into the icy water. I laughed. ‘Oh my God! It’s freezing. Why don’t you come in? Do you good.’

But he shook his head. ‘You’re mad. You know that.’

‘Catch!’ And I threw my sandals at him then, bent, cupped my hands with water and plunged my face into them, gathering up the water, splashing my face, eyes closed, splashing and splashing ritualistically, soaking my hair, my clothes. I was in the moment, as they say. In the moment. And I didn’t want to come out of the moment. Face dripping, I flung out my arms wide towards him as he stood there. 'Ask me to dance. Ask me to dance!'

He stared at me in a kind of disbelief, kind of astonishment, then he turned abruptly and walked back towards the meadow. For no reason that I could understand, I burst into tears. Yes, Mother: I was crying, crying. And they weren't quiet tears, but great gulping sobs that I couldn't control. Was it his turned back? Was it the moment of happiness ruined?

'It's just a family thing. Something I used to say to my mother.'

He heard me, and turned back and offered his hand as I got out of the water.

'Come on,' he said, and he put an arm round me as I sobbed so absurdly. I put my head against his shoulder as we walked.

'Sorry.'

He squeezed my hand.'Look, none of it was your fault, you know. You were never to blame for the children. It wasn't your fault.'

Not my fault? Not my fault? No one had said that before. Was it possible that I could be exonerated? Oh, the relief. The crucifying burden of responsibility began to roll away. Not my fault! I had to stop walking and I put my arms round him, buried my face and sobbed.

There was a low, distant rumbling of thunder and it began to rain intermittent, heavy drops. He took my arm and led me to the shelter of some trees. Together we sat against the trunk and I battled with the sobbing and gradually my body stopped quivering. After a moment, he touched my hand, just briefly. 'Don't be afraid to live,' he said. You can't help being alive, Rose. Let me ask you something. How is your foot? It's hurting, isn't it?'

I nodded; it was true it was aching.

'And so you can feel your foot all the time. You're aware of it being part of your body, because it's so painful.'

I was leaning against the trunk, one hand across my eyes. But listening.

'Look,' – and he leaned towards me. – 'when the damage to your foot heals and the pain goes away, does your foot cease to exist? Of course, not. Your foot is there, pain or no pain, is it not?'

'Yes, of course.'

'Rose,' – now he put his hand on my arm – 'it's the same with the pain of your grief. I understand that you dare not let it go. Who could? But I just want to tell you that the pain changes nothing, nor does the loss of it. Your children and your relationship with them will not cease to be true, real, present just because the pain goes away. Something from *The Prophet* says,' – and he quoted these beautiful words, which I have learned off by heart – '"When you are sorrowful, look again into your heart and you will see that in truth you are weeping for that which has been your delight. The deeper that sorrow carves into you being, the more the joy you can contain."'

He sat there looking at me

'Yes, I know it really,' I said, and the tears began again. 'But I want them here so much, you see. It's so lonely ... there's nothing else to cling on to, no one to help except them. They are the only ones who can make it all right – and there's this awful silence. Please—' I couldn't go on and we just sat there. After a few moments, I could say, 'Thank you,' and then, 'can't say any more now, but thank you. I won't lose them, will I?'

He said, 'When you let go of the pain, the silence will go, too. I think you have been struggling so hard, you were concentrating on the pain so much, you blocked out everything else.'

All I could do was nod.

He passed me his handkerchief. 'How about some lunch? There's a nice little place near here that does pub lunches and I don't know about you, but I could do with a drink.'

Chapter 38

I gave him a quick kiss on each cheek as we parted in the lobby and in return he patted me a couple of times on my arm, saying, 'Go on, go and have a rest. Glad you enjoyed the day, but you do look a bit weary now.'

I was tired, but it was not the usual tiredness; it was a gentle, a relaxed sort of tiredness, a sort of sit-in-the-sun-with-your-eyes-closed feeling.

We had returned in time for evensong, but I didn't want to go. I didn't even want to go for the evening meal because I wasn't the slightest bit hungry. I was agitated with excitement, uncertainty. Thinking, Was I going to find happiness?

In my room, I undressed and lay on top of the covers. I was floating on the bed, which felt soft and comfortable, thinking about the day. And Guy, his voice, his expressions, solemn and concerned, gentle and amused. Thinking of those lovely words, which I could then only remember in part.

I'd told him of my concern for Brother Joseph, how angry I felt about the rabbit being put into the old dog kennels, anger at their treatment of him. Life was hard enough for him, I thought; his rabbit brought him so much comfort and joy. Couldn't he, Guy, have a word with Father Godfrey? Couldn't he do something about it? Couldn't he? It was such a little thing to ask, and he had promised to think about it.

'I went,' I said. 'Last night. I think I shouted. Yes, I did, because suddenly I was outraged.'

He shook his head. 'Oh dear. You are hopeless.' But he was smiling.

Then I told him about the two brothers holding hands and kissing – yes, they were most certainly kissing – and his expression changed and he became somewhat thoughtful and said nothing.

'Who were they? What were they doing out so late?'

'Not sure.'

It was clear to me that he wasn't going to say more, so for once I didn't press it. And I didn't want to think about Guy any more. I kept whispering that he was not important to me at all; that I didn't need him or anyone. Ever. Ever. I didn't want the feelings I had. I didn't want to care.

Madly, I began to hit the side of the bed with my fist, whispering, 'I don't want you. I don't need you – just Dan and Fleur. Nobody else. Nothing else.'

Yet what had he said about pain? It was easy for him. I thought, Would they perhaps cease the crying I could hear so often at night if I was happier? Would that dreadful crying stop? Could they be happy if I was happy? Did I owe it to them? I could certainly try to be happy for them and enjoy things again for them, even to love for them. Fucking hell! I just didn't know what to do with myself. This nervous agitation, like falling in love, was worse than the pain itself, because I thought to be happy again was a betrayal. As if they didn't matter. And my frustration with myself, with everything and everybody, grew with the dusk.

I got off the bed and began wandering round the room, absurdly wishing I could be with Guy. I couldn't keep still; my insides were fluttering and restless and the room became a prison. I had to get out. I had to do something.

I had no thought of where to go or what to do. Nothing seemed satisfactory and I was beginning to be increasingly angry. Angry with myself, angry that I didn't know what to do, angry about

Joseph and the rabbit business. It was then I decided to go and check on the rabbit. It was just something to do. I went to fetch a cardigan, because for some reason it felt chilly to me, and then I made my way up the path and towards the Monks' Walk.

The avenue was longer than I remembered, and several times I turned to the left, expecting to find the path to the old dog run, but each time found my way blocked by hedges and bushes.

Despite a hazy moon, it was dark amongst the trees and I began to panic, thinking that I had gone too far and had somehow completely lost my sense of direction. Perhaps I would go around in circles until dawn. In my anxiety, I tripped on a fallen branch and cursed as the pain shot through my foot. I picked it up, intending to throw it to one side, but its thick solidity made me feel safer in the darkness, and I used it as a kind of walking stick.

Because I was nervous, I decided to turn back, thinking I would never find the run, when out of nowhere came a man's voice, and I grabbed the branch tightly, as a weapon. I had forgotten the brothers of the night before, and hoped it was Joseph talking to his rabbit, although it didn't sound like him.

I stood rigid and waited so I might hear for sure who it was. The voices again. Voices. Two men speaking. I heard the metallic twang of wire and knew they were by the run. Something wasn't right. Something odd was going on. I knew it, just had the feeling something would happen to Joseph's rabbit. God knows why.

Then all the fear went, all the uncertainty, and I moved towards the sounds, my branch at the ready for protection just in case, and I found myself in the clearing that preceded the run.

Who was there and what were they doing? If it was something to do with the rabbit, I was not going to stand by and do nothing this time. Not this time. I had failed to act before. Had just let things happen around me, but never again. Never would I just stand by. I could feel a kind of fury in me and kind of rage – for Joseph, for myself, a rage about life.

I hadn't screamed for Fleur to come out of the tomb nor unplugged all the tubes and taken Dan to the river. I had done nothing, just stood by and let them go. But not this time. 'Go on, Minch! Don't just stand there. Do something.'

It was easy to be quiet through the thick grass, and they were talking anyway. And there they were in the dim light, a shining bald head, arms outstretched – crucifix like- hanging onto the open wire gate, the shorter one gazing up at him. The rabbit was surely lost, gone.

'No, you don't!' I screamed. 'You don't. Not this time.' And I ran towards the Christ figure on the cross and, lifting the branch, brought it down with one mighty blow. Blow after blow. And they fell.

I screamed out, 'No you don't. No you bloody well don't. You bastards!' as all my pent-up grief exploded, until the breath was gone from me, and I sank to the ground and lay beside the other figures in the damp grass.

They found me inside the run, leaning against the wire fence. And in my arms, the rabbit, stunned also into stillness. The branch, now in two pieces, lay on the ground outside the open gate.

Out of the darkness stumbled Bertram, his head bleeding badly, as Brother Oswald raised the alarm. Trembling and shaking, he banged on Godfrey's door and, screeching, broke the news, before collapsing and weeping in his room.

Godfrey, still in his dressing gown, woke Guy and together they crossed the lawn into the Monks' Walk, taking great strides, hurrying without running, Guy carrying a medical bag. Towards them out of the dark, Bertram, groaning, lurched towards them, pushing Guy out of the way.

'Where is she?'

Bertram pointed towads the run.

'Can you manage to get back to the house?'

He nodded through his groans, his head hanging from his shoulders. He had lifted his habit against his head to stem the bleeding.

Chapter 39

Godfrey was overwhelmed. He sat in his chair, first rubbing his face in his hands and then closing his eyes with a sigh that became a low moan. 'Good God! What can have possessed the woman? Never in my entire…'

He looked at his watch: ten to three. Again, he exhaled a breath of exhaustion and his eyes lifted to the sherry cupboard.

He pulled himself up, robotically, and reached for the bottle and a glass. The opened bottle he left standing on his desk. Frightened himself, he downed the drink standing up. He knew he couldn't wait until morning to see Bertram again. He had to know if he intended pressing charges or not. At least he was alive! Oh God! The place would be overrun, what with the Philips man and now the police. He shuddered visibly. Whatever had come over her? Something possessed her. The last person in the world— Damn the woman! He should feel sorry for her, concerned – she was obviously deranged – but he was furious and panicking.

He turned towards the door, hitting his leg on the corner of the desk. He wasn't in control any more. No, everything was a shambles. If Wiltshire heard— He brushed his hair violently with his hand and left the room.

All the lights were on in the corridors and he ignored the mutterings behind the closed doors.

The light showed under Bertram's door and Godfrey knocked. His irritation was growing by the minute; he should feel sorry for him, but he did not.

Bertram was propped up in bed, a large plaster over his head, through which blood had seeped.

Godfrey remained standing at the end of the bed, challenging Bertram to look at him for, unusually, he was now avoiding Godfrey's eyes, while Godfrey could not disguise his contempt and some pleasure at Bertram's descent.

He studied the podgy figure, pale and ill-at-ease as he lay against his pillows.

'Are you going to bring charges or not?' Godfrey had no time, nor the will for niceties.

Bertram shook his head.

Relieved beyond words, Godfrey had difficulty in maintaining his severity, yet he desired to prolong Bertram's discomfiture.

'Why not? You are entitled to, I should suppose.'

Bertram's hand found the glass of water on the table beside him. It shook and some water spilled on the covers as he lifted it to his thick, flabby lips.

'What were you doing out, anyway? Rather late, wasn't it? Lights out and all that?'

Bertram replaced the glass, looked at Godfrey with some of the old defiance and shrugged. Godfrey made himself hold his eyes; never again would he allow Bertram to drive him onto the defensive.

'I can guess,' he sneered, and turned towards the door. But he hesitated for a moment before leaving. 'Good job the foxes didn't get that rabbit.'

Joseph was still on his knees, praying, when he heard the hurrying of feet, the talking, never allowed, the opening and shutting of doors, lights switched on. He peered into the corridor. Someone was in Brother Oswald's room. And was that crying? He wanted to help.

Then he heard the word rabbit. Quite distinctly. 'Rabbit.'

'Francis!' he choked aloud. 'The foxes have got Francis.'

He pulled his habit over his vest and, still in his slippers, ran, already breathless, down the stairs and out into the night, across the lawn and up the avenue towards the kennels. All the time uttering breathlessly, 'Francis! Francis.'

He tripped and crashed down and, unsteady as he tried to get up, his legs giving way, he fell again and now he began to cry, the tears from his red eyes dripping down his roughly shaven face.

'Francis, Francis. Holy Mother of God.'

With all his strength and willpower, he got up a second time, steadied himself as hastily as he could, and then half ran, half stumbled onwards, too breathless now to utter anything.

When, finally, he arrived at Billie's kennels, he saw a group of brothers. That's all he saw. He pushed past, gasping, choking, holding his chest as if to stop it from bursting open.

Someone caught hold of his shoulder, but he pushed away. Where did the strength come from? He cried out for Billie. Then someone took his arm and led him through the closed gate into the run and he saw the lady. She was sitting down and she had hold of Francis.

He fell to his knees with exhaustion and with relief. His nose was running now, as well as his eyes, his breath rasping. He couldn't speak.

No one spoke that he could hear.

'Francis!' When he had breath, he got hold of the rabbit and someone helped him to his feet, but still he couldn't speak, nor smile. Nor anything. He would carry Francis away.

They brought the box and walked with him. Was it Brother David?

Chapter 40

I can't remember exactly who helped me back to my room, but two people did. 'Get into bed,' one said as we reached my door. Then they left me.

At that moment, I wanted to die. Couldn't face what I had done. On the bed I curled up like a foetus, my head on my knees, my hands pulling my head down. I curled up so tightly, eyes shut, and kept repeating,' Oh! God. Oh! My God. Someone save me.'

I would come up for air, realise again the horror of what I had done and, knowing there was no going back, curled up again, back into the womb. Escaping.

I knew the police would come and I would have to go with them to answer questions. And then the court case would follow some time, and then prison. The fear was so bad, the shaking so uncontrollable, that, suddenly like some kind of self-defence, it turned to anger. Did I care? Was I sorry? I had to stand up for myself. It wasn't premeditated, I would tell them. But no! I was empowered, despite the fear. Bloody well served them right. Trying to let out the rabbit. Cruel beyond words. No, they had it coming to them. But not that way, not that way. Christ!

Guy did come briefly, looking pretty shaken himself, and gave me a sedative, simply saying he would see me in the morning.

The sunlight woke me because the curtains had not been drawn and when I realised that I was still dressed, I remembered. You know people talk about their stomach falling? Believe me, I felt I was falling through the bed. Terrified into rigidity. I cut myself off from it. I was a murderer. Please let me die. Scared to death but not sorry. At least I'd made a stand, just as I had when I threw my breakfast on the dining-room floor as a child, and when I chucked the pack of cards around my room because Mother was so unfair. I was afraid of what would happen, but not afraid of life any more.

The bells rang for morning prayer. I timed it, and then knew they were having breakfast. And I waited for Guy, who I knew would come, for he would have understood, not condoned, I'm sure, but understood that I needed him, so when at last I heard the knock on the door, I breathed, 'Oh, thank God.' But it was Father Godfrey standing just inside, looking awkward, his fingers rolling round and round.

I was waiting for him to tell me to prepare myself for the police.

'We won't go into it now,' he said, 'but Brother Bertram doesn't want any fuss, in any case. I know you—'

'He's not dead? You're not going to do anything? You're not going to call the police?'

He shook his head and I burst into tears, saying irrationally, 'Oh, please, please…'

'I know you were concerned about— It's lucky the stick was so brittle.' He appeared to be speaking to someone else. Not me.

He swung his arms back and forth, his long fingers, opening and closing into his palms . He looked thoroughly weary, and I was sorry.

'What can I say? Thank you. I don't know what to say. I'm not really like that.'

I was ashamed of my uncontrollable sobbing.

'So sorry for the trouble; I don't know what came over me. It was just—' I was going to go on about the rabbit and Joseph, but he held up his hand.

'I'm afraid we have been of little help to you. I'm sorry for that. But…' And he didn't finish his sentence. 'While I think of it, I've asked Brother David to bring you over some sort of breakfast. Mrs Gregory, as you know, we are leaving here in less than three weeks.'

'Yes.'

'Well as you can imagine we have more than … we have much to do.'

'I'll go home today if nothing is going to happen to me. Can I go? Can you let me go?' I saw him visibly relax.

'Do you feel up to driving? We could always—'

'No! No! Really, I'm fine.' But I was absolutely exhausted. 'Please say sorry to … sorry, I don't know his name.'

'Brother Bertram. And I suppose Brother Oswald as well; he's still in shock.' he muttered. 'Yes, well…'

He turned as if to leave, and then stopped. 'I think perhaps a short prayer is in order,' he said. 'Help to calm you.'

He stood by the door, arms by his side, head lowered. I hung mine and waited.

'May the peace of the Lord be always with you. And the blessing of God the Father, God the Son and God the Holy Spirit be upon you, now and for ever more. Amen.'

'Thank you,' I said.

He raised his hand and left.

He shut the door quietly, somehow obliterating his presence there. He was miserable. It was the sight of her. Pale, vulnerable. And as he walked down the path away from her, he was transported back to his dream and the garden in India and Padma. Pale and vulnerable.

I dressed quickly, waiting for Guy. It was Guy I needed then. Absolutely.

But Brother David arrived with a marmalade sandwich and a glass of milk. He stood in the doorway and I took the tray from him. I smiled; he nodded and then, pointing to the envelopes on the tray, said that Dr Guy had asked him to bring the letters.

'Can you ask him to come over to see me, please? I'm not feeling very well.'

'I think he's gone out.'

'Gone out?'

'I believe so. It's his day off.'

'Fine! Thanks for letting me know.' And I shut the door behind him.

One letter was addressed to my doctor and the other to me. He'd just written.

Dear [illegible]

The other letter is for Jonathan, as you can see. Go to see him as soon as you can, and good luck with everything. It's been difficult for you, but I'm sure everything will be fine in the end. Be patient! And do as you are told. Enclosed is a photocopy of those lines from The Prophet *by Kahlil Gibran.*

Guy

I screwed up the note and threw it in the wastepaper basket, [illegible] unfolded the sheet with the words he had recited to me. I read [illegible] and knew then that all I wanted was to go home.

But Joseph and the rabbit delayed me. He arrived with [illegible] on the lead, grinning. He pulled the rabbit into my r[illegible]

'Say thank you, Francis. Say thank you to the lady. [illegible] to say thank you,' he said. 'Don't you! Don't you?'

'It was my pleasure, tell him. Not long now, Joseph [illegible] will both be off on another adventure.' His face fell.

'I don't want to go. Not to leave Billie.'

It was quite spontaneous. I emptied out the jar [illegible] Guy had given me when I hurt my leg. 'Come [illegible]

It was quite spontaneous. I emptied out the jar of painkillers Guy had given me when I hurt my foot. 'Come on,' I said, 'I've

got an idea. Come on with Francis and show me where Billie is.'

'In the "graves" garden.' He giggled nervously.

I knew exactly what I was going to do.

He half ran, as usual, in front of me, dragging the rabbit behind him, and led me to an area on the right of the Monks' Walk that was like an overgrown garden surrounded by trees and with a dozen or so mounds headed by small gravestones. He stopped by one of these, which lay to the edge near the trees. 'Here,' he called.

I read the words: *Here lies Brother John, 1900–1978. May his soul rest in peace.*

The rabbit was nibbling the grass on the mound as Joseph stood watching me.

I took his arm. 'You know your friend, Billie, isn't really here, Joseph, don't you? He's where we all go when we die. And where they go when they die means I think that they can still be with friends and loved ones, in a different sort of way. And in a different way, we can be with them. They – you know the ones we don't have with us here on earth any more – only want us to be happy. I'm sure of that. He'll be with you, Joseph, wherever you are. That's good, isn't it?'

He was staring from me to the rabbit, from me to the rabbit. Then he nodded.

I showed him the empty jar. 'This may seem bonkers, but look, Joseph, you put a little bit of the grave into this.'

I held the bottle out for him and took the lead from his hand.

He hesitated. 'Take some with me?' And then he fell on his knees and began to scrabble at the earth with his long yellow fingernails, much like the rabbit's claws, to loosen the earth.

'Push some of that in,' I said.

He sprinkled the earth into the palms of his hands and held them over the bottle. The earth dropped in and around, but he continued until the jar was full.

'That's fine,' I said.

I took the bottle and screwed back the top as tightly as I could, while he struggled to get up, leaving an untidy, earthy patch on the grave ,which I tried to stamp down with my foot.

I put the bottle into my trouser pocket and took his arm to steady him.

'Where is it?' he asked and I gave him the bottle.

He shook it and stared at it, whispering something about Billie's grave, and then he put it in his habit pocket.

A grin spread all over his face. 'I can take him with me … just a bit?'

'It's just a reminder,' I said. 'Like a souvenir, kind of. Not exactly, but sort of, kind of.'

'He's not really there, Francis.'

'Billie is everywhere,.' I said.

I knew what I wanted to do next. I tied the lead to the wooden fence while Joseph stood staring at the grave.

'Come on,' I said. 'We have to celebrate. We have to dance for Billie. Dance round his grave. Come on, Joseph.'

And I took both his earthy, grubby hands, smelled his rancid, warm breath, saw the filthy habit but heard the laughter, the giggling laughter of a naughty child. And I began to pull him round the grave, side-step, side-step, gallop, gallop, gallop. He was bent double laughing and I began to dance and sing,

I danced on a Friday when the sky turned black –
It's hard to dance with the devil on your back.
They buried my body and they thought I'd gone,
but I am the Dance, and I still go on.

He did the best gallop he could and together we went around the grave holding hands, while the rabbit nibbled away at the grass.

Chapter 41

When I visited his grave, I was surprised to find the house in such a state. I don't know what I expected. I knew the abbey had been bought and was to become a hotel; I should have expected the chaos.

I had to park in the lane, as the area outside, where Guy and I had parked our cars, was blocked by builders' vans. They were expecting me and, unlike the first time, I was welcomed in by the new owner, Max Sinclair, who, wearing jeans and a T-shirt hanging loose, his hair ruffled and dusty with plaster, looked distracted.

The noise from drills, hammers and men shouting as the place heaved with workmen almost drowned out his voice. He looked momentarily irritated. He was with an architect, he explained but I was welcome to visit the grave and could I find my own way?

'We've had to do a bit of work over there,' he said and handed me a key. 'It's locked now. Sorry to be rushed.'

The entrance hall was empty of furniture and covered in dust, as were the French windows, one of which was open. I was sad and uncomfortable to see it all like that. The lawn was still the same and the cedar tree, and I could have cried to see the rope still hanging there. Then I wanted to laugh.

The rose garden had gone and in its place was a swimming pool, tiled in blue, now empty; it wasn't finished, for the paving around it was incomplete. I guessed the visitors' block would become changing rooms and showers, even a sauna, for this was going to be quite a hotel when it was completed.

The Monks' Walk had not been touched and I was sure it would be left for visitors to enjoy, much as the monks had done.

Everything around there was familiar. I didn't go to the dogs' run – couldn't face that – but went directly to the graveyard, which had been fenced in with high, sturdy fencing and the overgrown entrance cleared for a new wrought-iron gate, which was padlocked.

Inside was as untidy as ever, though; I was pleased about that. I wouldn't have like it to have been sanitised. Of course, I knew where the grave would be, and there it was, next to Billie's. Grass had not covered it yet; it was still just a mound of earth, but with the usual gravestone and inscription: *Here lies Brother Joseph, 1900–1983. May his soul rest in peace.*

'I've come to see you, Joseph. You are at peace now,' I said, 'and right here with Billie. What you wanted. You will be so very pleased about that. I can hear your chuckle! I hope you liked the cards I wrote you with the animal pictures. It was lucky to find the rabbit ones.

'Joseph, this will make you happy. I want you to know that I have Francis now. They let me have him. And I have the collar and lead, just the same. He's happy, Joseph, and so am I. He hops around the garden and around the house, though mainly the kitchen, but he does have a cage, just for night-time. Sometimes he sits on my lap. It's like having a cat! Can rabbits be like cats, do you think? Oh, Joseph, you would laugh. My house isn't lonely any more, the silences have gone and I don't have to have the radio on all the time.

'I am well, although I still have some medication; not pleased about that, nor pleased that I have to see a therapist every week, but she is good, and anyway it was Hobson's, because the doctor said it was that or hospital. So no choice, really. Anyway, it's all working and it feels right to come back here, too. I do believe now that God, whatever that is, is powerless but inspirational and loving.

We all know how difficult that is, don't we, Joseph? To love and be powerless. And it's true what Matthew said, that if we humans don't do it, it won't get done. But it's OK, I can move on now.

'Work is good. Busy, but that's good too. Oh – and I'm playing tennis again. Things are looking up. I'm only forty-one, and I expect, sometime, someone will ask me to dance!

'I have had a letter from Guy, by the way; he's back in general practice and happy, it seems. Not sure if I will see him again, but you never know.

'Now, Joseph, don't think me completely mad, but, besides these flowers, I have brought something from Francis. You'll never guess. Look!'

I took the little jar out of my bag, opened it and sprinkled the rabbit's droppings all over his grave. And the tears turned to bursts of laughter. Laughter.

'Bye, Joseph' – but it's never goodbye, really. I stood for a little while longer but then, job done, completed, I left for home.

A Note on the Author

Sylvia Colley was born in Eastleigh, Hamshire. She became an English teacher and spent many years as head of English at the Purcell School in North London.

She has published two books of poetry, *Juliet* and *It's Not What I Wanted Though* and a novel, *Lights on Dark Water*, to good reviews. Her poetry has been read on BBC Radio and a documentary *The Tale of Three Daughters*, about her life and work, was produced by Piers Plowright for Radio 4. She lives in Pinner, Middlesex.

Acknowledgements

Many thanks to Sarah and Kate of Muswell Press for wise advice and support.
To Kate Quarry for sensitive editing.
And to Piers Plowright for constant encouragement and help.